The Funniest Man in the World

The Funniest Man in the World

The Wild and Crazy Humor
of

Ephraim Kishon

SHAPOLSKY PUBLISHERS, INC.

Published in the United States of America 1989 by
Shapolsky Publishers, Inc.

Copyright © 1989 by Ephraim Kishon

First published in the United Kingdom 1989 by
PRION, an imprint of Multimedia Books Limited,
32/34 Gordon House Road, London NW5 1LP

Translated from the Hebrew by Johanan Goldman and Miriam Arad
Cover illustration by Itzik Rennert

All rights reserved under International and Pan American
Copyright Conventions. No part of this book may be used
or reproduced in any manner whatsoever without written permission
from the publisher and copyright holder, except in the case
of brief quotations embodied in critical articles
or reviews

For any additional information, contact:

Shapolsky Publishers, Inc.
136 West 22nd Street, New York, NY 10011
212-633-2022

9 8 7 6 5 4 3 2 1

Library of Congress Cataloging-in-Publication Data

Kishon, Ephraim
the Funniest Man in the World:
The Wild and Crazy Humor of Ephraim Kishon
1. Wit and humor. 2. Ephraim Kishon.
ISBN 0-944007-47-3

Typeset by Wyvern Typesetting Limited, UK
Jacket origination by Reprocraft 87 Limited, UK
Printed in the United Kingdom by Bath Press Limited

Enjoy!

From
Denise Bschente

Contents

THE TRAVEL BUG 9

A GONDOLA FOR TWO 16

LAND WITHOUT FLEAS 22

THE COATHANGERS OF VIENNA 27

BULLSHIT ARTISTS 31

THE CHAMP CHUMP 37

TAXI GYMNASTICS 39

PUNCTILIO 44

MY CLIENT, MR. KITCHEN 47

JEWISH POKER 54

THE ESPRESSO GAMBIT 58

CASTOR OIL DAY 60

BEWARE THE GUARD 62

CHOP STORY 64

A SEAFUL OF MIRACLES 66

NOW IT CAN BE TOLD 69

THE GREAT FLIGHT 73

BORN TO BE FREE 78

THE JERUSALEM GOLEM 83

2 × 2 = SCHULTZ 88

MAXIMALISTS' REVOLT 93

STAMPING OUT 97

THE QUIZ 100
THE PHILHARMONIC COUGH 105
COUNSEL FOR THE DEFENSE 108
THE BEDSIDE MANNER 113
WHISTLE STOP 117
CAREFUL, SHALOW WATER 121
FUHRMAN PAYS 125
THE HARDEST CURRENCY 131
PEANUTS FOR THE MASSES 136
THE ECONOMICS OF BABY-SITTING 140
THE PLUMBER 145
TSVINJI PEES 148
THE INSULT AND THE INJURY 152
HAIR 156
THE JOYS OF FAMILY TRANSPORT 161
THE FOUR HORSEMEN OF THE APOCALYPSE 164
THE LAST OF THE CRAFTSMEN 169
WIDE-OPEN SKIES 175
LIVING OUT OF A SUITCASE 179
A WIFE FOR IZZY 181
THE BLAUMILCH CANAL 185

The Travel Bug

Traveling abroad has become a common pastime all over the world. In Israel it is an obsession.

There are many reasons for this state of affairs. First of all, it is hot in our country, almost as hot as in New York, and most of the time you feel like a dried prune. A time-honored local adage goes like this: "If you start looking like your passport photo, it's high time you went abroad."

Israelis, they say, are more entitled to travel than other people. Firstly, one should remember that the greater part of our population was not born here, but voluntarily chose this country as their fatherland, so it is only natural that they should hark back to the old country now and then, to compare things and check whether their choice was a wise one. Besides, by now we know every speck of dust on the 12,000 or so square miles of our mini-land. If a tourist boasts to us about his plan to start exploring the country over its whole length and breadth on the morrow, we ask him: "And what are you going to do the day after tomorrow?"

But the main cause for our urge to travel abroad is, beyond any doubt, the Government's opposition to it.

This attitude of our Government is rooted in a number of considerations, both spiritual and practical. Firstly, Jewish common sense dictates: why travel? who needs travel? isn't it nice here? Secondly, the Bible – which somehow always sides with the Government – explicitly states that the Lord punished Cain after the painful incident in which he got involved by turning him into a tourist: "A vagabond shalt thou be upon the earth," whereupon Cain sighed, "My punishment is greater than I can bear." Thirdly, from a strictly economic point of view, the Government considers tourism a boon – as long as it is one-way, that is from the outside inward. The other direction leads to perdition. Just think of it: that Israeli citizens should go and squander the little hard currency they earn by the sweat of their brow – and in the very places the money came from! That may be likened to a mendicant soliciting donations in a delicatessen and rightaway spending them on goose-liver pâté....

Small wonder that the Government looks askance at the fugitives: "You want to travel abroad, hey?" it asks. "Why not. This is a free country. If you are not ashamed of yourself, go right ahead! But we'll clap such a travel tax on you that you'll sell your last shirt to pay for it...."

And so with the onset of the hot season Operation Last Shirt starts. And everybody travels. It is said that the frustrated Government's secret agents are patrolling the tourist playgrounds of the world, leaving behind warning messages for Israeli traitors. Be that as it may, it is a fact that one of the Ionic columns on the Acropolis features an inscription engraved in well-formed Hebrew characters:

Snob! Have you been to Tiberias yet?

However, for purely technical reasons – mainly the lack of suitable means of mass transportation – the *whole* population cannot leave Israel during the summer months. The fate of those leaving is therefore that of a persecuted minority.

I first came across this phenomenon when I told our neighbor, a certain Felix Selig, about our decision to hop over to the Continent during the summer months. I disclosed our plan to him as to a friend, so that he might be a partner to our joy. But his reaction was quite unexpected. He blanched, leant heavily against the wall and his breath came in gasps: "That's nice!" he whispered hoarsely. "Where to, if I may ask?"

"Rhodes," I answered, "Italy, Switzerland, France, England, maybe the USA...."

"Is that all?" my neighbor sneered, trembling in his whole body. "Bon voyage, *sir*!"

With that he turned his back on me. I was shocked. Had I

offended him in some way?

Next day I tried to apologize to Selig, but he ignored my greeting and crossed to the other side of the street. The lady from upstairs came up to me, her eyes blazing: "Is it true?" she hissed. "Where to?"

"Rhodes," I replied, "maybe Italy as well."

"*Very nice!*" the lady said. "Goodbye, *sir!*"

Clearly a sort of social boycott was taking shape all around us. So for a few days I went into hiding and kept out of the public eye. Then I met the neighbor from the ground floor in the courtyard.

"A week in Rhodes," I quickly threw at him. "A week . . . Rhodes . . . only a week . . . only Rhodes. . . ."

"*Only?*" he huffed. "So go!"

To my great relief he did not sneer "*sir!*" Apparently I had struck the right tone. During the last week before our departure, I told those who asked where we were going: "Just fishing, to the seaside."

That passed, somehow.

It was quite clear to us *why* we were traveling, on the other hand we were ignorant of *how* to go about it. For a decade we had lived in Israel without leaving it even once. And now we felt like the eaglet leaving the parental eyrie for the first time and worrying itself sick whether its wings will carry it, whether its engines will break down, whether it will run out of the little hard currency it has been allotted.

What has to be done?

Somewhere in the outskirts of Tel Aviv there is a little grove in which there lives a very old owl, who is said to be a fount of wisdom acquired during endless peregrinations. He has been abroad numberless times, has experienced many hardships and customs inspections. If anyone at all in this whole world could help us, he could.

By the way, the old owl's name is Lipshitz.

One Saturday morning we drove out to the grove. Lipshitz was sitting motionless on a gnarled tree branch, only his clever Jewish eyes blinked from time to time.

"Master," we poured out to him our anxiety. "How? When?

Where from? Where to? Why?"

"Take a seat," said Lipshitz, and slipped into his hole in the tree to make tea. Then he came back and gave us an object lesson in globetrotting: "Many people think," he opened, "that money is everything. They are right. Not so much because of high prices, but rather because you can't get loans abroad. Don't say, 'I'll make a few bucks there somehow or other', because what makes you think you can make the Gentiles part with even one dollar?"

"Rabbi," I said, "I can sing."

"Son," said Lipshitz, "stop that nonsense. Take all the money the Treasury is ready to provide you with, secure it with a safety pin in an innermost pocket and don't touch it except for buying food, and even that circumspectly! Never, but never, go to a restaurant where you are served by more than one lean waiter, or where they light candles under your plate, because you'll have to pawn your last shirt to pay the check. For the same reason, never – you hear, never! – order a dish which figures only in French on the menu. If you see hard-boiled eggs appearing as *canapés d'oeufs durs au sel à la Chateaubriand*, beat it as fast as your legs will carry you!"

"Rabbi," I interrupted, "it's not to eat that I'm traveling. I want to have a good time."

"I know," the wise owl Lipshitz blinked his eyes. "Let's take the attractions one by one, in the order of their importance. Are you taking your wife along?"

"Yes."

"That's one off. There remain: the scenery, the theater, museums and family invitations. The scenery is almost free, except in Switzerland where you pay a minimum fee of 1.50 Swiss francs for every cubic meter of air at sea level and progressively more as you go up the mountains.

"The theater should be no problem. All you have to do just before curtain time is step up to the well-dressed gentleman biting his nails in the foyer and speak to him in quick-fire Hebrew, interspersing your monologue with words like 'artist, critic, studio', until he becomes convinced that you are an Arab theater man and gives you a free ticket. This trick does not work in striptease joints, where you have to pay, but there are occasions when even I don't economize...."

Lipshitz fell silent for a while, then continued: "If you come across two stone lions as you walk the streets of a big city, enter without hesitating; you'll find yourself in a museum. Once inside, don't follow your intuition, but rather join the first group of tourists being shown around by an experienced guide. Should the guide throw a furious glance at you, look back at him just as furiously. At the conclusion of the museum tour, you may board the group's special bus and sightsee all over the country with them. But remember: never go to a museum without taking two days' rations along! It has happened more than once that careless visitors got lost in the cavernous halls of the museum, could not find the way out and starved to death. At the British Museum, for instance, they discover human skeletons at every spring-cleaning.

"What's left? Oh yes, family visits. Believe me, they are no fun at all and cost a fortune, because you have to buy flowers for the hostess and go home by taxi."

"Dear Master," I said, "all this is wonderful, but for the time being I'm still at the packing stage...."

"Then pack wisely," Lipshitz warned me. "Don't take many suitcases, because in every single country a new suitcase will join your luggage, even if you don't buy a thing. This is a strange, inexplicable phenomenon, yet an indisputable fact. Upon your arrival at a railroad station, hire a porter *right away*, taking care not to show your inferiority complex. That is much wiser than dragging your suitcase half the way – only to hire a porter when on the verge of a physical breakdown....

"At the hotel always check in advance whether the tip is included in the price, but under no circumstances do your haggling in the language of the country. Why should you stutter and stammer? Let *him* stutter and stammer! Thus, in Paris speak English, in London French. In Greece speak only Hebrew, because they know all the other languages...."

"Speaking of hotels," the old owl continued, "don't forget to take with you a few 200-watt light bulbs. Strange as this may sound, the lighting in even the most luxurious European hotels is so weak that you can hardly read even the most screaming headlines. Since it is forbidden to cook and eat in your room, you'll have to make special arrangements for the inconspicuous removal of leftovers. I suggest you knead a solid ball out of the remnants of your supper, which you can then toss out of the window at midnight. A more difficult task is to introduce the ingredients needed for cooking. Milk bottles are especially tricky. You can smuggle them in in an oversized doctor's bag or in a violin case. Don't hide the electric hot plate, on which you do your illegal cooking, in your suitcase. A snooping chambermaid may find it while cleaning your room. Hide it in the clothes closet where they never clean...."

"All right, Lipshitz," I said, "you talk, talk about everything, except the main thing: how much does one tip, whom and when?"

"You'll never know for sure," the owl announced. "As a rule, at the restaurant you have to tip ten per cent of the check, at the theater fifteen per cent of the usher's collar size, for information on the whereabouts of a certain street – five per cent of the informant's age. To be on the safe side, keep tipping until he looks happy. This rule is especially valid for taxi drivers. Always pay when both you and your luggage are safely on the curb, otherwise the irate driver may kidnap your belongings."

"And," Lipshitz added, "don't you ever forget that you are not a human being, just a tourist. Don't be fooled by outer signs: the natives' bows and curtsies refer only to your status as milch cow, source of quick profits. As a person, they hate your guts, and if you are fluent in their language that increases their instinctive dislike of you sevenfold...."

"That's that," the sage owl wound up. "Last but not least, don't fly. Travelling by ship you will avoid the worst calamity a mortal tourist can experience: I am referring to those tense moments when the luggage of *every* passenger on your plane has been piled up in the customs shed of the airport . . . only you stay empty-handed at the foot of the conveyor. 'No more suitcases, sir, not even one. Yours were sent by mistake to Cairo. . . .' Strong men have been known to turn gray in moments like these. Go by ship, son, go by ship. So at least you'll have a week's rest before the ordeal. . . ."

☐ *Contrary to hearsay not every newly married couple has a good time in Venice. To tell the truth it is not so easy to get along in that fabled city. The unwary step off the train and straight into a lagoon. For the city fathers of this antique burg, foreseeing the plague of traffic accidents, laid it out on the sea, replacing streets with canals and completely banning wheeled traffic.*

A Gondola for Two

―――□―――

We asked the man behind the station information desk how we could get to the hotel, taking into consideration that the little woman is a somewhat weak swimmer.

"Take a taxi," the official suggested. "In front of the station you'll find any number of motorboats. The main thing," he added, "under no circumstances hire a gondola, because they are terribly expensive...."

We threw a confident "leave it to us" at him and moved out with our luggage. We didn't spy a single motorboat along the quay, only fleets of gondolas, their oarsmen lounging in the stern dressed in blue-striped T-shirts, their eyes burning with greed. We said to ourselves, "What the hell," and hailed the nearest gondola. An old man with a pole helped us to sit down in it for 100 lire, while a good-hearted youngster stored our luggage under our feet for 200. A third one said "go" for 50....

The trip was most enjoyable, in spite of the embarrassment every Israeli *has* to feel reclining on velvet cushions while his fellow man is exerting superhuman efforts rowing. The pleasure-craft itself resembles the Vikings' long boat, in which those hardy pirates invaded and subjugated Western Europe. Clearly, gondolas had been invented while slavery was still legal and suitcases unknown. Yet, in all fairness, we must admit that our Viking kept gaily singing: "*O sole mio* ... !"

The wife was deeply moved by the romance of it all, and had she not feared for the safety of the suitcases with the straw bags in them, would have burst into sobs. I kept thinking of how much our Viking would overcharge us, seeing that he put on a great show of heavy breathing, and prepared thoroughly for the impending battle: "*Amico*," I would tell him, "you came to the wrong address! Maybe you can cheat greenhorns, but not me, old boy...."

"Two thousand lire," the gondoliere announced as we dropped anchor on the doorstep of our hotel. "*Due mille!*"

"*Amico*...."

Whereupon he started shouting and cursing, *molto* suitcases, *molto* tired, nine *bambinos* at home and Santa Maria della Croce! It was terrible to see man in his primeval anger. I quickly threw the ruffian 2,100 lire, an expression of deep scorn on my face, and unloaded the suitcases.

Then what?

Then the man pushed this affluence into his pocket and went on smiling his queer smile....

"*Arrivederci* to you!" I roared, "What the hell are you waiting for, if I may ask?"

"A tip," the man fluted, "a little tip, signor, if you don't mind...."

"Now look here, old boy," I lost my temper. "Let's be reasonable, all right? After all, you not only blackmailed me for two thousand lire, but out of sheer habit I threw in another hundred, didn't I?"

"Yes," said the Viking, "but that was an official tip. It's customary to give an ordinary tip as well...."

Without another word, we turned our backs on him. We gave him only 50 lire more. The hotel porter who had witnessed the scene from a distance asked me why I had not hired a motorboat – did no one tell me that it was madness to hire a gondola?

"How much did he squeeze out of you?"

"*Squeeze* out of me?" I asked. "Fifteen hundred lire...."

The porter winced. In a little municipal booklet he showed me the official tariff: "800 lire for a pair of lovers with eight suitcases."

However, part of our expenses were refunded at noon in a restaurant. An old lady at the table next to ours dropped her fork. Remembering my Old World manners, I picked it up. She slipped me 200 lire. "*Grazie*," the wife said, grabbed the money and stuffed it in her handbag. After a while she remarked that the old bag had not been too generous. . . .

We shall be charitable and not say anything about the cost of restaurant meals. After all, one has to pay for two waiters with gold braid on their snow-white uniforms standing permanently at the back of your chair, and for the luxury of having the chef in person pour oil on your salad from an antique crystal decanter. Never mind, we said, one has to eat, but we won't spend another penny on gondolas in Venice.

We fell only once more into their clutches. It happened after we had paid a brief courtesy call on the local Jewish ghetto. Tired by the walking and depressed by the shades of Shylock, we dragged ourselves along the canal which bisects the city, and somehow the idle thought occurred to me that, after all, in view of the special circumstances, perhaps. . . .

Before you could say Giovanni Robinson we were encircled by about a score of armed Vikings who had apparently read my hidden thoughts. They barred all our escape routes, so in the end I chose the navigator with the kindest face. (The others dispersed amid atrocious cursing.) Before we boarded his boat, I asked the vital question: "*Quanto costa?* How much?"

"Nineteen hundred. . . !"

I showed him the municipal booklet with the 800 official lire, whereupon the man was seized by uncontrollable guffaws, so that I began to fear for his life. We turned our backs on him. After all, it wasn't so far to the hotel, just a pleasant walk. . . .

"Thirteen hundred," I said. "My last offer. . . ."

"Seventeen hundred and fifty!"

"All right," I said, "but that's the total and final price, including all the supplements, taxes, insurance, oar levy and babysitter, right?"

"Right, *signore*," the Viking replied, unruffled. "Seventeen hundred and fifty and not another bean."

The gondola slid over the murky waters in tense silence. In spite of all our precautions, we were worried and kept wondering: *where was the trap?*

The little woman broke the silence querulously: "What's going on here," she said, "why doesn't he sing?" With that she turned to the oarsman: "*S'il vous plaît, O sole mio. . . .*"

"*Prego, signora*," the Viking answered, and promptly the beautiful song rose to his lips. The sweet melody put us in a sentimental mood, as if something long bygone, something intrinsically good, had suddenly mellowed the raucously mercenary bustle of the tourist city, which . . . which . . . which. . . .

Almost simultaneously, the blood froze in our veins.

"My goodness," the wife whispered hoarsely, "*I have asked him to sing!*"

By now it was too late.

"Three thousand," the Viking said calmly in front of the hotel. "Seventeen hundred and fifty is the all-inclusive price for the ride, twelve hundred and fifty for the serenade. . . ."

The wife, that naïve child, threw herself on the gondoliere with daring bred by despair, and asked him why was that song so expensive?

"*Specialista!*" the man explained pleasantly. "*Tenore! Molto* strain for the voice, *molto* muscle, *molti bambini* (7), *Santa Maria*. . . ."

He got 150 as a joint tip and not a lira more. There is a limit, after all. The Viking took his spoils and sailed off gaily, singing "*O sole mio. . . .*"

After this, we swore we would never again sit down in a gondola. Naturally, our situation became more difficult as the days passed since the rumor had spread like wildfire all over the city that a crazy couple had arrived who were willing to pay any price for a gondola ride.

Almost every day, there was a matitutinal knock at our door: "A *bello* tour all over the city, *soltante* two thousand six hundred and fifty!"

By then we had also stopped eating in restaurants. The problem of alimentation without the benefit of gold-braided waiters had been happily solved when we discovered one of those huge automats so popular in progressive Europe, and on it the legend: "Insert 100 lire for a toasted cheese sandwich *à la Milanese*." Providence had come to our rescue! I inserted 100 lire and out popped a note: "Another 50, please! Welcome to sunny Italy!"

I put in another 20 lire. A sandwich came out wrapped in cellophane. It was divine. Gratefully I put another 10 lire into the automat and a note came out: *"Grazie!"*

On the day we had to leave for Switzerland we took no chances and ordered a motorboat well in advance of our departure. We were ready even to pay more, only not to enrich those pirates.

The motorboat did not show up.

I don't know why. It simply did not come. These things sometimes happen in Italy. Half an hour before the train was due to leave, we ran like crazy along the sewer in front of our hotel: "Gondola!" we shouted, "Gondola!"

Nothing.

No gondolas. Now there weren't any gondolas. Not even one. They had disappeared. Evaporated. Vanished. Gone. At the very last moment we discovered, right under our noses, a doddering old man napping in a gondola. We hurried down the steps and woke him:

"*Presto!* Quick!" we gasped. "To the railway station! Hurry!"

The old Viking lifted his drooping eyelids. His eyes flashed 5000 accompanied by the loud and clear ring of his built-in cash register.

We missed the train!

Breathing heavily, we tottered over to the admiral in charge of the railway station and asked him when was the next train to Geneva.

"Geneva?" said the admiral. "At 5:30."

"Haha!" I laughed into his face. "Four at the outside!"

"5:15!"
"4:20!"
"Five and not a minute less!"
"4:30 so help me, only for you...."

After some more haggling, we settled for 4:45. I gave the admiral a small consideration and that left me only 50 lire for the locomotive driver. Thus we departed Italy, without a penny to our names, but not later than 6:23.

☐ *They speak three languages in Switzerland: the Germans know French and Italian, the French know French and the Italians know how to work the land. Those of French origin look down upon the Germans, the Germans look down upon the French, both look down upon the Italians, and all three look down upon foreigners.*

LAND WITHOUT FLEAS

Before going out on our first walk in Zurich, we had a quiet talk with the hotel porter: "They say the Swiss don't even lock their bicycles," I gushed to the porter, "but just leave them out in the street. Is it true?"

"Of course."

"And," the wife asked, "aren't they ever stolen?"

"Of course they are. And how! But anyone who doesn't lock his bicycle deserves to have it stolen. Now, when the city is full of foreigners...."

Every fifth person in Switzerland is a foreigner. I was No. 1,100,005, my wife was No. 1,100,010.

All the same, there are Swiss emigrants. Even Israel gets a few genuine born-Swiss citizens. Why? I don't want to be obvious, but I think it's because of the cleanliness. One day, for instance, we went to the famous Zurich Zoo and stopped in front of the monkey cage.

As is known, the favorite pastime of mamma chimpanzees is to hunt for fleas in the fur of their offspring. Well, this mamma chimpanzee had been looking for over half an hour for any sort of insect on the head of her little son: she scratched, combed, rummaged about in his hair, then gave up, an expression of total dejection on her face, and sat down to brood.

"We don't even know what to do," the keeper complained. "We

even imported fleas, but they fled in the face of Swiss hygiene. How is it going to end?"

I had no advice for him. I told the keeper that soon I would be back in Israel, and lectured him about our rich, flourishing insect life. When we parted, he had tears in his eyes.

We first clashed with the supernatural cleanliness of the country on the famous Bahnhofstrasse. We had gone into one of the department stores lining the street, taken the escalator to the fourth floor, and bought two precisely crafted cream puffs packed on trim little paper plates. On the way down we opened the package, and walking to our hotel, swallowed the cakes greedily. They were great. We had never eaten such marvelous pastry before, except in Italy a day and a half ago. But hardly had we swallowed the last bit when we heard a big helloing and someone came running after us: "*'tschuldigung*," a well-dressed gentleman panted, "you lost your plates."

With that he held out the chocolate-stained paper plates together with the wrapping paper, which we had thoughtlessly tossed away at the climax of our enjoyment.

"*'tschuldigung*," I replied to our benefactor, "we haven't 'lost' this. . . ."

"Then what?"

"What do you mean, then what?"

"Then how come I found it on the pavement?"

"*Tanke schön*," the wife said quickly, took the sticky papers from the gentleman's hand and dragged me away.

"Have you gone out of your mind?" the little woman hissed. "Look around!"

I looked around and reeled with the shock of it. Only then did I realize that we were in clean Switzerland's cleanest city and in that city's most antiseptic quarter. On the sidewalks there was not a trace of litter; at worst there were a few pale stains which had not yet come out in the scrubbing. In the distance an impeccably dressed sweeper kept chasing a few lazily rolling dust specks. And I had dared to pollute this immaculately clean pavement with my dirty paper! It was sacrilege!

I carefully folded the paper plates in such a way that the sticky parts faced inward, then looked around, greatly perplexed.

"All right," I said, "still I can't carry this on me wherever I go. After all, we'll be in Switzerland for two weeks...."

"Keep your shirt on," the little one calmed me. "Somewhere we'll find a place where there is litter, so that we can dispose of the plates legally."

She made this statement at 11 A.M., and by 2 P.M. I was still in possession of the gooey things. If we had found but one tiny slip of paper, we would have unhesitatingly mated our bundle to it, but we did not find even a piece of confetti. In the end we boarded a streetcar, sat down in a corner next to the open window, and at a curve, deep in conversation, instinctively, with a careless flick of our wrist....

Screech!!!

The driver slammed on the brakes.

"*Tanke sehr!*" I nimbly jumped off the streetcar and picked up our lost valuables.

"Very kind of you," I thanked the conductor as we moved off again. "Luckily nothing has happened to them...."

By then we were ready to press the panic button. With the courage of the desperate I accosted an elderly Swiss gentleman sitting next to me, and asked him what would he do if he were stuck with, let's say, a piece of dirty paper and would like to get rid of it. The old gentleman thought it over for a moment, then said this sounded so hypothetical that he could scarcely visualize such a situation but, theoretically, he supposed he would take the paper waste in question home and on Sunday afternoon burn it. I disclosed to him that the package in my possession qualified as waste, whereupon the Swiss gentleman immediately gave us his address, inviting us to bring it there next day at 3:45, and once there, we could stay as his guests to the end of the year – his wife would be delighted.

My wife visibly felt inclined to accept the invitation, but I had my doubts about its sincerity, so while expressing our deep-felt gratitude, I told him I would take advantage of his kind offer only in an emergency as I had thought of a simpler method for getting rid of the nuisance: I would put it in an envelope and mail it to Israel.

"All right," said the old gentleman, "but what are they going to do with it there?"

"They'll throw it into the Jordan," the wife said, whereupon the old gentleman nodded understandingly, and after a sentimental farewell we got off in the suburbs. My idea was to wait for the fall of darkness and then bury the bundle under a tree. However, we found all trees girdled with iron fencing, to prevent the burying of refuse. . . .

We strolled back toward the centre of the city and there, to our delight, hanging on a lamp post, discovered a cute little litter basket with an inscription reading: "Keep Zurich clean, drop your refuse here!" At the end of our tether we stumbled over to the basket and with a relieved smile dropped in our infamous burden. . . .

"*'tschuldigung*," a policeman remarked behind our backs, "kindly take that thing back! This is a brand-new basket. Let's keep it clean!"

"But," I said in a daze, "but it says here to drop your litter in."

"The litter, yes. But no refuse!"

I stuck in my arm to the elbow and fished out the little parcel. A strange heat flushed my cheeks and my teeth started chattering.

"Listen," I croaked to the little one, "I'm going to eat the damn thing!"

"Don't be silly," the saintly woman replied, "you won't take that abomination into your mouth."

"All right," I whispered, "I'll have it cooked. . . ."

Just then we were passing an exclusive restaurant, so we walked in and ran into the headwaiter, who immediately noticed the little parcel.

"Waste paper?" the headwaiter asked. "Shall we cook it?"

"Yes," I muttered. "Well done, please. . . ."

"The usual way," the headwaiter said, then placed the Thing on a silver platter and hurried away to the kitchen. Fearing the worst, I fidgeted about on my chair, because the cooking in Swiss restaurants is rather colorless. Ten minutes later, a waiter brought in the little parcel:

they had fried it, then smothered it in dill sauce. I took a bite and spat it out.

"It's burnt," I shouted, "disgusting!"

With that we jumped up and left.

Before our mind's eye there appeared good old Rothschild Boulevard in Tel Aviv, with the brilliant sunshine of our country pleasantly reflecting itself in the thousands of nice heaps of glittering litter.

The Coathangers of Vienna

Winter is a serious affair in Vienna. Anyone who goes outdoors without an overcoat on his back runs an excellent chance of subsisting on aspirin for the next few days. However, as soon as you enter any place of public entertainment, a silver-haired Austrian grandmother shoots up out of the ground and says, "*Garderobe.*"

Which is "cloakroom" in Deutsch. With that, she takes your overcoat and drags it to her lair, never to be seen again except on your way out, against a ransom. As a matter of fact, she doesn't ask for money, she only returns the kidnapped coat and says, "*Danke schön.*"

Once, in a big Vienna theater, I asked the local crone, "How much do I owe you?"

She answered, "The usual."

That is, she isn't interested in the remuneration; she doesn't do this for the money but for the excitement. She is a fixture of the Austrian capital; she is one of Vienna's famous coat removers.

The single-minded devotion of the Viennese coat remover is proverbial. A fly cannot get into one of the city's restaurants without removing its coat.

Once, if memory serves me, I intended only to say a word to an acquaintance in the renowned Sacher patisserie. I dashed past the hag on duty, but before I had reached the end of the hall she barred my way.

"*Garderobe.*"

"Just a moment, ma'am," I threw at her and continued on my way in. "Only a word, *bitte.*"

She blocked my further progress. I jumped aside to bypass her, but she dived and caught my coat. I shook her off and skillfully dribbled past her. Then she caught me in a running tackle and held onto my knees with her two hands. It was a brief but bitter struggle. You wouldn't believe what powerful, sinewy arms these old women have. She impounded my coat, with a few deft dabs cleaned me of all traces of the fight, and hung the coat carefully on a hanger. Then she stuck a number on the coat and handed me a counterfoil bearing the same number. I pushed the slip in my pocket, went into Sacher's, shouted "Eight o'clock!" at Friedrich, turned on my heel, took out the slip and gave it to the old lady. Thereupon she took the coat off its hanger, removed a few strands of invisible lint from it, as well as the number, and said, "*Danke schön.*"

I gave her ten schillings, a fortune even by international standards, meaning to bribe her so that she wouldn't stop me next time, but she accepted the gift with equanimity.

As I said, for the Vienna removers, money is only a means, not an end. One has only to look into their tired eyes framed by a sallow and covetous face to realize that they live for their daily coats. Take away your coat from them and you have taken away their *raison d'être*. It's a sort of addiction, like hashish.

It once happened that a group of irate citizens organized themselves and burst into a hotel all at the same time, dispersing like lightning with all their coats still on their backs into the far corners of the building. In such emergencies the old monster divides herself into three or four submonsters and shows up in every corner, and collects the contraband coats one by one, saying, "*Garderobe.*"

I saw with my own eyes a respected aged Austrian poet swallow hard and refuse to surrender his coat. He buttoned it right up and clutched it to his shrivelled body with a strength belying his years, like the clerk in Gogol's story "The Coat".

"I won't," he bawled and pursed his bloodless lips. "I'm sick. I'm running a temperature. I don't want to."

The overripe hat-check girl stood behind him mutely for a whole hour, never for a second removing her eyes from the object of her lust. In the end the distinguished poet broke down and handed over his coat peacefully. One could smell violence in the air.

"Why?" I asked my hotel manager. "Why do they remove everyone's coat?"

"Don't know," the man answered, his eyes shifting nervously. "Bringing coats in is forbidden."

"But why?"

"They might get crumpled."

They are everywhere, the grandmas of Vienna. To the end of my days I shall remember the time I was sitting in a posh cinema and suddenly felt a light tug from below. The old lady had crawled under the seats up to my coat and now breathed into the darkness, "*Garderobe.*"

What is the solution? It is said that a Latin American tourist, badgered half out of his mind by the Viennese coat brigade, one day wrapped his naked body in a fur coat, only to be unwrapped by the old lady at his hotel and left in the altogether in the middle of the crowded lobby. The old lady handed him his number without batting an eyelid and placidly hung up his coat.

How does one combat such fanaticism? One night, in a fit of uncharacteristic recklessness, I burst past the old crone of a central hotel and succeeded in jumping into an elevator and soaring up to the sixteenth floor.

"*Garderobe*," the old lady whispered, standing ramrod straight in in front of the elevator door on the sixteenth floor. Personally, I was badly winded, while she was only blinking. She folded my coat carefully on her brawny arms and scuttled down into her hutch. What a remarkable species!

The day before my departure from the capital of the Hapsburgs I was awakened at midnight by a sudden crash. The door of my hotel room was smashed in and fell off its hinges. The old woman burst in and made straight for the closet. She took my coat out together with its hanger.

"Sir," she hissed, "kiss it goodbye."

Naturally it was only a dream. In the morning my coat was returned undamaged at the downstairs cloakroom. The number 107 was still sticking to it.

☐ *To the best of our knowledge, no one ever asked for the minority opinion at a bullfight — that is, nobody is interested in hearing how the bull feels about it all. It seems that this is a first attempt in this field and, of all people, it had to be undertaken by a Hebrew writer. Or could it be that this is no mere coincidence?*

BULLSHIT ARTISTS

The *corrida* is a national institution in Spain, just like the eating of steaks in Texas. The two are even related, but the Spaniards like their steak on the hoof. The charging bull therefore becomes a daily commodity and even the unofficial arms of the state. Small wonder then that we had hardly landed in beautiful Barcelona when we excitedly asked the first customs officer we ran into, "Is any *corrida* still due to take place?" "*Sí*," the man answered, "the last one this year. You lucky bastard!" It appears that with the arrival of the rains, Spanish bulls heave a sigh of relief, and we had arrived just before the gates of the arena were to be locked up for the winter.

"You don't know how lucky you are, señor," the sons of Catalonia said to me, their eyes flashing. "Miguel is in town!"

This sounded most encouraging: Miguel. My old acquaintance, a respected Barcelona lawyer, bought us a couple of very good seats, exactly beneath the ornate box of the honorary President, who would signal Miguel with a special handkerchief when to slaughter the bull. At least 60,000 sports- and meat-loving aficionados were crowding the monster stadium. Half of them were American tourists and one a perplexed Israeli. The atmosphere was extremely tense. Everyone realized that the clash between the bull and Miguel was inevitable. Raven-haired, demure señoritas were waving their fans, and in their beautiful eyes one could read genocide. We went on chewing gum placidly, but our emotions were in a turmoil.

"Look!" our lawyer called. "Miguel!"

Into the arena stepped a brigade of cavalry equipped with light arms, followed by the matador's personal aides, and finally Miguel himself, who was very lean and resplendent in embroidered silks. He bowed deeply to us and we gave him the thumbs down greeting. In the meantime my lawyer checked the program, stopping at the list of bulls, which featured names, weight and marital status.

"My God!" he whispered. "These are very dangerous bulls!"

I asked him whether he hated bulls. My lawyer reflected for a while, then assured me that he did not hate them, although he despised them for their morbid aggressiveness toward toreadors. I inquired of him what would be the fate of a pacifist bull who refused to fight. It seems that such conscientious objectors are deprived of all civil rights. A good-looking cow is ushered in and she promptly draws the shlemiel out of the arena. Such a miserable bull as this has to wait months, figuratively pawing the ground with impatience, before he gets another chance to be butchered.

Luckily our bull was carved from sterner material. He stormed into the arena and immediately charged the red cloth waved by the picadors or whatever you call them. These did not lose their cool but scattered in all directions and jumped the fence in mortal fear. A storm of protest arose all around us. Men jumped to their feet and shook their fists at the bloodthirsty beast, while the women threw kisses to the innocently persecuted picadors.

"What the hell are you charging around for?" my lawyer yelled at the bull. "Who do you think you are, you sonofabitch?"

The bull stopped in his tracks and squinted up at us.

"What are you staring at?" the lawyer roared. "Charge, damn it!"

The bull lowered his horns and rushed a beribboned attendant.

"Stop him!" my lawyer shouted. "This bull is a murderer!"

And indeed it was quite an ugly sight that a bull should be so hostile toward mankind, just because he's being stabbed from all sides, and spears, hooks and national flags are being stuck into his flesh.

Look, now his horns have almost touched one of the sportsmen, who has done him no harm except wave a red cloth in his face. The audience is seething with hatred; the lynch atmosphere grows ever stronger. Reinforcements thirty-strong flow into the arena, armed with pikes, armor and automatic weapons. The management's first helicopters appear over the arena carrying air-to-surface missiles. The bull stops, hugging the wall and breathing heavily.

"You coward!" my lawyer shouts. "Is that how they taught you to fight?"

The bull raises his eyes to him. "I want to fight?"

"Yes, you!" the lawyer replies and turns to the butchers. "Kill him, boys, kill him quickly; otherwise by the Madonna of Seville I'll come down there myself!"

In the end, self-discipline gained the upper hand and he did not go down. The women started throwing kisses at the armored knight who had entered the arena to a fanfare of massed bugles.

"Is that Miguel?" I asked.

"No. The bull is not yet tired enough," my neighbors explained and poured their scorn on the goings-on below. "Come on, buster, you miserable cow, let's see what you can do now!"

Several more took to jeering, "Cow!" The bull lunged at the horse and toppled it on its rider.

"Police!" the bleachers echoed. "This is not a bull. This is a public menace!"

"Attack innocent horses, will you?" My lawyer jumped to his feet. "This is where you die, you creep!"

It was evident that the bull could not stand lawyers. Actually, by now he could hardly stand on his feet at all and was clearly suffering from a bad case of persecution mania. Personally, I decided to look at matters from his point of view and found that it was a sadly depressing situation: foreign soil, a hostile audience, overwhelming numerical superiority. But it was too late in the day for philosophical meditation. The women threw kisses with increased energy. Miguel returned to the arena with orchestral accompaniment, in his hands an oversized sword.

He was wearing an elegant cape and exuded health and vigor. At first he went through a number of classic exercises with the red cloth he was carrying, while the audience sighed with pleasure. Every time the bull punctured the air with his horns, Miguel shouted, "*Olé!*"

He also kept taunting the bull.

"Where are you, bully boy? Now show us what you can do! Oops, baby, oops! You just try to touch me and I'll make mincemeat of you, so help me, *olé!*"

The women showered him with flowers. Miguel drew his sword and prepared for the dignified ritual slaughter.

"The sword must pierce the lungs, kidneys, heart and intestines," my lawyer exclaimed, "with a single stroke delivered with great virtuosity."

Miguel rose on his toes like a ballet dancer and stuck the blade into the trembling beast's back. But he must have pierced only two or three of his targets, because the bull did not drop to his knees. Quite to the contrary, he seemed to have recovered somewhat. The mob's raving hatred overflowed all bounds.

"Hey, what's the matter?" they roared at the bull. "Drop dead immediately!"

My lawyer rolled his program into a bullhorn. "Malingerer!" he shouted. "Behave like a man, you rotten chicken!"

The bull was properly fed up. He stepped up to the President's box. "Sir," he shouted, "if you don't take this louse off my back I won't play bull!"

The President waved him away. "I don't talk to bulls! Kill him!"

Miguel rose to his full height, raised his sword, and in a flash a whole division of reinforcements burst in to madden the enemy for him. I realized it was difficult to overcome the bloodthirsty beast as long as he could stand on his own four legs. So they threw at him another twenty darts, poisoned arrows and tear gas.

"This is the end," the lawyer predicted. "Now he'll get his comeuppance!"

It turns out that if the torero kills his bull skillfully enough the

President makes him a gift of the bull's ear. Should he do his job with a brilliance beyond the call of duty and should the slaughter be absolutely outstanding, he gets the tail as well. The toreros are Spain's most admired millionaires. Men are happy to touch the fringes of their jackets, women send them love letters and toreros learn to read them at night school. They are true acrobats, these brave Miguels, as they stand erect, stalking the raging monster who is at the end of his tether.

"Now you'll see something," my lawyer predicted. "Miguel will drop to his knees and execute a brilliant veronica. That is, at the very last moment he will move aside with devilish skill and thrust his sword into the heart of this maddened beast."

The band played a gay march, then came an ominous roll of drums. Miguel dropped to his knees and the bull charged him according to plan. At the last moment Miguel moved aside. So did the bull. Miguel sailed through the air and landed spread-eagled on the hot sand.

The spectators' patience had run out.

"Enough," they shouted at the bull. "What brutality, you sadist!"

Some spectators were calling for a doctor. The bull rolled Miguel in front of him with much feeling, then he lifted him on his horns and tossed him high above his head.

I jumped to my feet: "*Olé!*" I shouted at the top of my lungs.

My lawyer darted a murderous glance at me, but by then nothing could stop me.

"Bravo!" I roared. "Let him have it! Don't spare the creep!"

I blew kisses at the brave bull, and when the legendary Miguel arced through the air for the third time, I tore up my program and scattered it ecstatically. Then I threw my necktie, my shirt and a shoe at the victor. According to some witnesses I even sang the march from *Carmen* in a falsetto voice. But at this stage more reinforcements tore into the arena, headed by two armored cars and fresh toreadors with drawn swords. I could stand it no longer, took leave of my downcast lawyer, and fled. As I passed under the colonnade on my way out I heard the victory roars of the crowd and I understood that at long last they had succeeded in knocking off the bull with a concentrated barrage of mortar bombs. The toreador probably got a tail and a half, while three tired nags towed his victim outside. On the other hand, I also saw the great Miguel placed in an ambulance, and that made me feel better. I grabbed the first taxi and made straight for Tel Aviv, to my little sons who will never become toreadors because of their red hair. I'll just have to reconcile myself to that, once and for all.

□ For a while we had a good mind to award the title of the biggest fool on earth to the Cypriot guide who took us touring and couldn't find the road back, whereupon he burst into tears and said: "But I swear it was still here yesterday!" Then the laurels passed to the Israeli traffic cop who tagged on to us on location in Herzliya and wanted to know the name of the film we were shooting. We said Sallah, and the cop wrinkled his brow and thought hard: "Sallah?" he mumbled. "Ain't seen it."

Now the record has been smashed. In Barcelona, Spain. A courteous hotel porter has won the title hands down. I was ringing from my room to Reception, and he answered in what he took to be English. The conversation belongs to history.

The Champ Chump

———□———

"I'm planning to fly to Madrid tomorrow," I told the porter. "I don't speak Spanish, so would you kindly book me a hotel room with bath?"

"You wait, I check," said the porter, and went off and came back and said: "Sorry, sir, we no having room free here. You try next week," and hung up. I rang back: "You got me wrong just now. I'm not looking for a room here, but in Madrid."

"Sorry you take all big trouble call from Madrid, sir. We no having free room, you try next week."

"Una momento!" I shrieked. "I'm not in Madrid. I'm just looking for a room in Madrid."

"Sorry, sir, this hotel not in Madrid, sir. This hotel in Barcelona."

"I know. I'm staying in it."

"You staying?"

"Yes."

"And you not happy your room, sir?"

"I'm perfectly happy my room, but I've got to fly to Madrid, as I said."

"You want I take down your luggage, sir?"

"Not now. Tomorrow."

"Very good, sir. Good night," and he hung up. I rang back: "This is me, the one who's flying to Madrid tomorrow. I'm asking you again if you could get me a room with bath."

"You wait, I check," said the porter, and went off and came back and said: "Sorry, sir, all roomses here booked. You try...."

"I don't want a room in *this* hotel! I've already got one! I'm in 203."

"Room 203? Sorry, sir, ledger here say that room booked."

"Sure it's booked! I'm staying in it!"

"And you want change it?"

"No. I'm leaving for Madrid tomorrow. So could you get me a room?"

"For tomorrow?"

"Yes."

"You wait, I check," said the porter, and went and came and asked: "With bath?"

"Yes."

"Ah, then you lucky, sir. I found room for you tomorrow."

"Thank God."

"Room 203 coming free."

"Thank you."

"You welcome. Anythings else, sir?"

"One lime juice."

"Coming up, sir."

Taxi Gymnastics

The French are a strange lot. One may admire them – they're so gifted and display such a marvelous command of their exquisite language; one may despise them – they're one and all a pack of conceited scoundrels; but one thing one cannot do – get a Frenchman to like you.

Whoever you are, the French will loathe you to a degree unsurpassed in the annals of man's inhumanity to man, simply because you are a miserable, tawdry, execrable, odious, crummy little foreigner who, to top it all, may be rather proud of the way he speaks French.

One feels the first whiff of this abhorrence at the airport. It's called after de Gaulle, on account of its length probably, and covers an area of several square miles which harbor one solitary baggage buggy named Suzanne. Millions of tourists make the air pilgrimage to Paris each year, so it's easy to imagine the animosity caused among them by the said Susie day in and day out. *And* she squeaks. But credit where credit's due, Squeaky Sue prepares one for all the myriad joys in store for one at the hands of Paris's taxi drivers.

Should the revered reader already have experienced the delight of visiting the Seine metropolis, then I will spare myself further explanation; if not, explanation is not going to help.

The streets of Paris are literally peppered with taxis – there are more taxis in Paris than fleas on a French poodle – the exact opposite of lone Sue at C. de G. But one can never catch one of the peppery fleas; they're all taken always. And should by some propitious circumstance a cab prove to be vacant, the driver will refuse to take you because he doesn't like your face. Paris is probably the only city in the world where the cab drivers are physiognomists of Olympic standard.

Taxi drivers in other parts of the world can on occasion be choosy and demanding, it's true. In New York, for instance, a special law had to be passed obliging every cab driver to accept *all* fares regardless of color, creed, or presumed purse potential – provided of course that he is not on his way to dinner. For this reason New York cabs have a special hunger light on the roof. It automatically goes on if the driver is on the lookout for a bigger spender than you appear to be.

In France they don't need a light on the roof. They spot you a mile off. The average taxi-driving Parisian can immediately tell if you're a lousy tourist or not, if you're toying with the idea of asking him to drive you out into the countryside (in which case, God help you), if your hotel is situated on a busy street and, above all, if you are of a generous and giving nature or just another American.

So you stand there on the *trottoir* flailing away like a one-armed windmill, catching up on the gymnastics you failed to perform that morning. The first five cabs will sweep past without batting a blinker. As a rule the sixth will screech to a halt beside you, but the driver will be holding all four door handles in a vise-like grip.

"Where to?" he'll mutter out of the corner of his mouth, the corner with the cigarette in it. Whatever you reply, he will undoubtedly say, "*Merde*," swear that he has pressing business in the opposite direction and shoot off again. He says this on principle. The truth is that he can't stand you. For he is a taxi driver, and you, in nine hundred and ninety-nine cases out of a thousand, are not. You are a crummy tourist toad.

At first I thought there must be some arcane code that forbade Parisian taxi drivers to accept men wearing waistcoats or *not* wearing glasses – or was it a moustache you had to have? After a worrisome week I realized that they act according to one sole criterion: they won't drive *you*. Period.

One balmy French spring day I had just finished the obligatory thirty minutes' flailing on the damp Champs Elysées when along came No. Six with the standard, "Where to?"

Soaked to the skin and shivering, I stuttered, "Wherever you like, I leave it to you."

"That's not on my way," he spat, and was gone. They see through you straight away, these Gallic cavaliers. The man knew instinctively

TAXI GYMNASTICS

that the moment I set foot in his carriage I would start making demands and expressing a desire to be taken to some specific address. So I changed my tactics; I applied my intuition and attempted to guess his destination – I had no wish to be a nuisance, after all. On one memorable occasion I was almost successful.

It happened like this: I had a ticket for the opera one evening and had been doing my exercises for the prescribed half-hour when up screeched a typical Jean-Pierre, stuck his cigarette-chomping sourpuss cautiously out of the half-lowered window and grated, "Where to?"

And all at once it happened. My spirit guide was standing there right beside me. "He's going in the opposite direction to the opera," a small voice whispered in my ear, and I knew exactly what I had to do.

"Montmartre," I said coolly.

Jean-Pierre raised an astonished eyebrow – he knew full well I was headed for the opera – and said, "Jump in."

This was the day I finally got to ride in a real Parisian taxi. No matter how, or where to, I was in one. I leaned back in the mature upholstery and wallowed in *bonheur*. Even today, I distinctly remember the bliss that transported me for days on end thereafter and made me forget the hour-long footmarch through the precincts of nighttime Paris after having sat through an excruciatingly obscure play in an airless subterranean theater instead of going to the opera. No matter. I, a humble tourist pig, had been driven by a genuine Paris taxi driver. No one could take that away from me.

The price had been a high one. I had stumbled out of the wretched theater, stood there in the moonlight on the outskirts of Montmartre flailing away as usual, yelling and mumbling, praying in Hebrew and cursing in Hungarian, all to no avail; all the taxis ignored me. After an hour of supplication, I was still trudging along on foot. At three in the morning, I sank to my knees in the middle of a boulevard and began to cry. It got me nowhere, of course – they weren't born yesterday; every Parisian chauffeur knows the cheap trick with the tears and the kneeling down.

At dawn I staggered into my hotel. "The next time you come to

Paris, monsieur," the night porter said, "choose a hotel which is closer to the theater you wish to visit."

And then, one ineffable day, it came to pass that the very first cab I hailed stopped right beside me. The fellow must have been inebriated or something for he also took his hands off the door handles, allowing me to jump inside and triumphantly yell the name of the cinema I wished to be taken to.

"Tssss," Marcel hissed at the rear mirror, "that's off my route. Can't help you there, sorry."

I budged not an inch. We sat there eyeing each other in total silence for some minutes, then Marcel switched off the engine, got out, leaned through my open window and blew cigarette smoke into my face. "The motor's died on me. Get out, *cochon*."

I still can't think what got into me, but I remained firmly where I was. Very frightened, it's true, but quite resolute. "Then see if you can get it going again," I hissed back. "I'll wait."

Marcel was visibly impressed and immediately switched to emergency tactics. "Look here, monsieur," he appealed to my better nature, "this taxicab is my livelihood; I have a wife who is accustomed to luxury, several voracious children, and an aging concubine to support. If I drive you over to your lousy cinema I'll never find a fare on the way back and be forced to drive empty for miles on end. So be a good despicable tourist and shift your butt."

I remained steadfast – he was a good head and shoulders smaller than me.

Marcel shrugged and disappeared into a bistro on the other side of the *rue* and sat in the window sipping Pernod. I sat there completely immobile, determined to see it through, come what may. Capitulate? Not on your life.

An hour went by. Finally Marcel came back, eased himself behind the wheel, started the motor effortlessly and drove me smoothly to my cinema. He had clearly accepted me as a worthy opponent and decided to throw in the towel. I gave him a handsome tip. Of course I only caught the last ten minutes of the movie I wanted to see and was again obliged to spend most of the night flailing and trudging back to my hotel, but it was worth it. I had experienced a pinnacle of triumph as never before in my entire life.

My last day in Paris also brought me my last brush with its taxi drivers. The man who almost ran me down in Montparnasse shortly after midnight had no intention of allowing me to voice a preference as regards destinations. "I'm not going north," he informed me around the sopping cigarette end, "nor will I go south. If you're thinking of the area around the Arc de Triomphe forget it, and as to the size of my tip I warn you here and now that it's the middle of the night and—"

"Don't worry your dear head," I interrupted him, "here's ten francs for your trouble. I prefer to walk."

He fingered the proferred banknote as though it were contaminated. "*Merde*. You call that a tip?" he growled, stuffed my *merde* into his pocket and swept off.

I love them. I can't help myself. I'm addicted to Parisian taxi drivers.

☐ *The self-control and manners of the dwellers of the British Isles never fail to amaze the foreign visitor. I shall never forget the day when, at a London railroad station, a very fat man tried to board our chock-full train. He pushed and shoved, freely making use of his elbows, trying to make room for his great bulk and three suitcases. In our country, someone would long ago have knocked out some of his front teeth, but these well-mannered Englishmen were placidly watching the performance of this wild bull, their glances saying: "Such doings are below our dignity." At long last, an elderly gentleman remarked to our bullish friend: "Why are you pushing, sir? Others, too, would like to sit."*

"I don't care about others," he replied and went on bulldozing down the passengers. "Because of you, I'm not going to stand on my feet till Southampton."

No one argued with him, no one said another word. They ignored him and let him sit all the way — it is practically impossible to make an Englishman lose his temper. Our train was going to Birmingham, a destination diametrically opposed to Southampton.

PUNCTILIO

———☐———

And now, as a practical example of traditional British manners, may I describe my visit, or rather the leave-taking I took after my call at the Government Department for the Consolidation of Cultural Relations or Something. The Director General, Mr. MacFarland, had received me most cordially, treated me to tea, and now was personally seeing me to the door of his office which, naturally, was very high-ceilinged and panelled in iron-studded oak dating back to 1703. . . .

There, in front of the open door, we stopped.

"Please," MacFarland motioned, "after you, sir."

But by then I had spent two days on British soil and had become acquainted with the ways of civilized people.

"No, no, Mr. MacFarland," I did not budge, "only after you."

"Only after you, sir," MacFarland smiled. "This is my office, I'm at home."

"Age before beauty," I joked. "Only after you, Mr. MacFarland."

Thus we marked time and argued as to who was to be first across the threshold. As a matter of fact, I was in a hurry, but hated to hurt MacFarland's feelings, because he really was much older than I, and a British citizen to boot.

"No, no, Mr. MacFarland," I said to him and gave him a light shove, "only after you."

"Only after you, sir," MacFarland reacted, grabbed my arm and propelled me towards the exit. "I'm at home here."

"You are older," I replied, grabbing him by the shoulder and pulling him towards the door. "Only after you, Mr. MacFarland."

"I . . . I'm . . . at . . . home. . . ." MacFarland gasped since he was choking under my arm, but suddenly he put out a leg and tripped me. The unexpected fall put me in a precarious situation, but at the last moment I got hold of the table leg and thereby prevented MacFarland's moving me from my position.

"No, no," I grunted as I freed myself with great effort, "only after you, Mr. MacFarland."

My left coat sleeve had come off in the struggle and the Director General's pants had burst at the seams. For a while we glared at each other, panting. Suddenly, MacFarland rushed me, but I jumped aside and he crashed into the filing cabinet.

"Only after you, sir," MacFarland rose from the floor foaming at the mouth and swinging a chair over his head.

"No, no, Mr. MacFarland, only after you," I gasped and seized a heavy poker.

The chair sailed over my head and smashed Churchill's photograph into smithereens. I hurled the poker against the ceiling fixture and the light went out.

"I'm at home, sir," MacFarland hissed threateningly in the

darkness.

"But you are older," I replied and hurled the table in the direction of his voice. MacFarland screamed and fell in a dead faint to the ground. I groped my way over to him, got hold of his body and rolled it out into the corridor.

Naturally I rolled it in front of me over the doorstep, because I know what good manners demand.

☐ *Why muck around writing all our life, we said to ourselves, when all you have to do is sell a brilliant idea to a Hollywood producer and live in affluence for ever after, you and your children's children.*

We therefore booked a seat to the film capital of the world, determined that on the way to Los Angeles we would somehow find that brilliant idea our lucky descendants would refer to until the end of time as "the great turning point."

MY CLIENT, MR. KITCHEN

———☐———

My seat mate on the plane was a well-preserved native who, once airborne, fell into deep and sonorous slumber, most effectively vacuum-snoring my brain of all ideas.

Since the future of my progeny was at stake, I had no choice but to awaken him. Over Chicago I shook him lightly and said, "Pardon me, when are we arriving?"

"Dunno," he mumbled communicatively, "why?"

"Nothing," I answered. "You live in Hollywood, sir?"

"No."

"Then why are you going there?"

My neighbor opened one puzzled eye.

"Do I know?" he said. "Ask my agent! You have an agent?"

"No." This practically knocked him off his seat.

"But Good Lord," he exclaimed, "how are you going to live without an agent? Who's going to take care of you?"

"Dunno," I stuttered, "the Lord...?"

Only now did I realize why my neighbor's sleep was so sound. The cushion under his head was bigger, into his cup they had put two tea bags instead of one, and once, through my half-closed lids, I spotted one of the hostesses surreptitiously slipping him a pear. Clearly a mysterious force was at work here. Soon enough the nature of this force was disclosed. Over the State of Texas the hostess handed him a cable: "Message for you, Mr. Maxwell."

"Weather hot in Hollywood," his agent wrote, "put on gray pullover stop Dinner with Paramount President at 8:45 Kisses Joe."

"See?" my neighbor said. "That's all you need. A good agent!"

Then he embarked on a panegyric of the American agent as a national institution. According to him, the agent's task is not limited to pullovers and pears and such, but expresses itself mainly in the field of career and publicity; that is, the good agent extols, exalts and boosts his client's personality on sea, in the air and on land, using all the means of modern technology, until his last breath or the exhaustion of his budget, and may God bless him for his pains.

I was deeply impressed by Max's words. I asked him what was his profession.

"I'm an agent," he replied. "Why?"

I really didn't know why. Somewhat embarrassed, I asked him why, if he himself was an agent, as he said he was, did he need an agent, damn it.

"Perhaps you are a bad agent?"

"I'm a high-class agent," my neighbor allowed with a tolerant smile, "and that is exactly why I need an agent of my own. I cannot introduce myself everywhere: 'I'm the world's greatest agent.' Someone's got to say it for me and that's why I keep an agent. See?"

By the time we made Los Angeles, I was green with envy. Hardly had we touched down when the loudspeakers started blaring: "Mister Maxwell is requested to proceed to the blue Cadillac outside." A thickset man was waiting at the entrance with a bunch of flowers and an umbrella. Faithful Joe! There he was carrying the luggage to the Cadillac. Oh, Maxwell! I was left with my suitcases, abandoned and apprehensive, without an agent, without hope. I walked up to the information princess: "Could you help me find a hotel?"

The princess fluttered her exquisite and expensive eyelashes: "Didn't your agent," she asked, "make a reservation?"

"I haven't got an agent," I admitted abjectly, my lips tight and bloodless, "but I'm entitled to an hotel, aren't I? Could you recommend one?"

"There are two good agents living on my street," the princess mused. "Perhaps one of them would receive you even at this late hour, I can call him. . . ."

"I don't need an agent," I choked, "a hotel is what I need."

The hostess was utterly confused and gave me up as a bad job. I picked up the phone and at random dialed the Beverly Hills.

"Sorry, Mr. Kitchen, we got no rooms," the Desk replied curtly and hung up. I dragged my body and my lead-heavy suitcases to a taxi and ordered the driver to take me to a hotel. The driver started up: "Which hotel, mister?"

"I don't know."

The driver looked at me compassionately.

"No," I said to him, "I haven't got an agent, I simply haven't."

"That's very bad," said the driver, "because here you're sunk without a good agent. Look, even I got this night job through my agent. During the day I am a dish-washer. . . ."

He asked me why, as a matter of fact, didn't I have a good agent of my own. A matter of principle, I explained; I hate good agents mortally. Ever since birth. It's congenital with me. No agents.

"If that's how you were born, that's very bad," the driver allowed. "No one can live in Hollywood without an agent."

"I'm a famous writer," I pointed out.

"They won't even speak to you. . . ."

Los Angeles is the world's most sprawling city, Hollywood is at the other end and West Coast drivers are notoriously talkative. As we drove along I began to understand the agent syndrome in all its ramifications. Close, familial, sometimes almost incestuous relations exist in the City of Celluloid Dreams between the handful of artists and the ever-growing legions of agents. Only a few days ago, the driver related, the papers had been full of stories of a famous movie director who had strangled his agent in a fit of jealousy when the agent had dropped him in favor of a couple of flamenco dancers. He'll end in the electric chair, the director, the driver assured me. The jury would return a verdict of guilty, because murdering your agent is worse than patricide, because you are born to your father as a baby, while the agent adopts you in your maturity....

"Very interesting," I said, "but I'd like to get off here!"

As we passed the Beverly Hills I caught sight of the famous blue Cadillac and standing before it was no other than Faithful Joe in person. Surely, this was a sign from Heaven. I sprinted up to him and introduced myself, breathless: "Joe," I whispered, "take me!"

Joe looked me over dispassionately and slowly extracted a notebook from an inner pocket: "Nine-thirty A.M. tomorrow, TV interview at CBS," he said. "At 1:15 you meet Heda Hopper, the gossip columnist. At 2:10 luncheon with the President of Paramount Pictures. At 3 P.M. the photographer; don't forget your guitar...."

"Yes," I said, "but I'm not a pop singer."

"Let me handle these things, will you," Joe bridled. "Your room number is 2003. Breakfast at 7:30. Two soft-boiled eggs. They are good for your voice. Goodnight. Nice to have met you."

"Thank you."

"Just a second," Joe said. "Sign here!"

He pulled out a form covered with fine print. I threw a quick glance at it: on the territory of the United States, on the territory of the British Empire as it was in 1939, anywhere else in the world, I undertake to pay my agent 10 percent of my gross income, regardless of whether I earned it through work, a legacy, games of chance or from an honest finder's prize.

"Joe," I asked in a shaking voice, "is this for a lifetime?"

"What else?"

"Then, sorry," I threw at him and suitcases in hand started at a run toward the hotel lobby. Joe shouted after me not to bother, they wouldn't give me a room, but now no foreign agent in the world could stop me, because I had grasped the principle at the very last moment.

"I'm Bernie Schwartz," I stepped up to the desk. "I'm the agent of Mr. Kitchen, literary consultant to the President and author of *War and Peace* by Tolstoy. A double room with TV and be quick about it."

From the double room I called up Heda Hopper. "Hiya, Heda darling," I said to her. "I work now for Kitchen. You're sure dying to hear about this fantastic writer." With the President of Paramount Pictures I fixed for Friday. I promised to bring along a few scripts by the fabulous Kitchen. In a matter of days I established marvelous contacts and built up an amazing career for that nincompoop. Fortunately no personal problems arose, since no one wanted to meet me, preferring to deal directly with my agent. So after a week I came to the conclusion that I was completely superfluous here and fired myself peremptorily. I don't need a writer. What I need is a good agent.

☐ Now is the moment of truth, time to confess: this writer adores crooks. Actually it's not surprising, since the professions of humorist and swindler are quite closely related: they both depend on people's stupidity for a living. They both thrive on bureaucratic fuddledom, on troubles at home, on people's inability to think for themselves, on their vanity and hypocrisy, on the failings of the individual and society. The crook and the humorist are two intellectual criminals, the one in deed, the other in word; the one universal, the other international; two rogues, and brothers under the skin.

Personally I've admired the professional con man since childhood, and to this day I furtively keep my fingers crossed whenever Interpol are chasing some gifted master swindler around the globe. I remember for a fact that while other kids dreamed of flying to the moon or defeating one-eyed pirates in noble duels, in my childhood fantasies I sold old bridges on the Danube to venerable gentlemen.

The reason why I never progressed beyond childish hoaxes is not due to any particularly high-minded moral outlook on my part, but to the fact that I simply didn't have the nerve for the real thing, the paying swindle.

It's a pity really, because my natural curiosity about people and the various manifestations of their herd instinct has made me fairly adept at the con game. I must have been about ten when I discovered that we could collect a considerable crowd if a few of us juvenile delinquents stopped on a street corner, turned our eyes skyward and stared at a point in space. In time we got rather more ingenious. Once, as a high-school brat, yours truly went to the local amusement park with the mafia of his class. We took the ghost train through the Cave of Horrors, got off under cover of darkness in mid-cave beside some screeching owl or dangling skeleton, and proceeded to slap the cheeks of all our fellow travelers on the train as they came by. God, did we enjoy ourselves!

Then there was the occasion I'm still a bit ashamed of when I addressed my classmates as follows: "Anyone who feels like a double portion of vanilla ice cream after gym – stay in the room."

Half the class stayed. I counted them carefully and noted with satisfaction: "H'm, more than I thought."

The mob asked where was the ice cream.

"What ice cream?" I said. "I was only interested in the statistical aspect of it," and promptly fled for my life.

And the telephone! Ah, the possibilities provided by that devilish instrument!

Like my unforgettable evenings with Mathilda. Indefatigable teenager that I was, I would get out of bed in the middle of the night and ring up our next-door neighbor. He'd mumble a sleepy "hallo", whereupon I'd whisper his wife's name into the receiver in my deepest, sexiest voice: "Mathilda?"

"Who's that?" our neighbor would yell into the phone. "Who's that there?"

Click!

I'd hang up, and sit back to enjoy the tremendous row between Mr. and Mrs. Mathilda on the other side of the wall. They'd go at it with true Shakespearean gusto, and I'd listen and learn plenty about Life. Yes, those were the days. At sixteen I exchanged passionate love letters with middle-aged Lotharios who had responded to a little ad I'd put in the paper: "Young lonely widow seeks partner for life, preferably one she can consult on how to invest her money."

Such were my first literary efforts. Not long after, during the dark Nazi era, the trickster in me perfected his art to the point of saving my life for me — but that's another story for another book.

Now I have passed the baton to my enterprising friend Ervinke, who does all the things I feel a bit too old for myself. I honestly admire Ervinke, though I admit he's a bum. I'd even go so far as to call him an idle bum, but he's got a brain buzzing with bright schemes for turning human weaknesses to good profit for himself. Where the hell does he get all these ideas, I sometimes wonder, seeing that I invented him, Ervinke. He's taken on a life of his own now and thumbs his nose at me, his begetter.

JEWISH POKER

For quite a while the two of us sat at our table, wordlessly stirring our coffee. Ervinke was bored.

"All right," he said. "Let's play poker."

"No," I answered. "I hate cards. I always lose."

"Who's talking about cards?" thus Ervinke. "I was thinking of Jewish poker."

He then briefly explained the rules of the game. Jewish poker is played without cards, in your head, as befits the People of the Book.

"You think of a number, I also think of a number," Ervinke said. "Whoever thinks of a higher number wins. This sounds easy, but it has a hundred pitfalls. *Nu!*¹"

"All right," I agreed. "Let's try."

We plunked down 5 agorot² each, and leaning back in our chairs began to think of numbers. After a while Ervinke signaled that he had one. I said I was ready.

"All right," said Ervinke. "Let's hear your number."

"Eleven," I said.

"Twelve," Ervinke said, and took the money. I could have kicked myself, because originally I had thought of Fourteen, and only at the last moment had I climbed down to Eleven, I really don't know why.

---

¹The interjection "Nu!" – somewhat like the English "Well!" – plays the role of Jolly Joker in the Hebrew language. According to a superficial estimate, it has about 680 meanings, depending upon the speaker's facial expression and the time of day. Here are a few meanings picked at random:

"Come on!"

"Please leave me alone, can't you?"

"I didn't understand a word of what you said. What on earth are you driving at?"

"All right, suppose things are as you say, though mind you, I don't say you're right. Is that sufficient reason to start shouting as if I had trod on your corns? Bloody fool! Yes, you. Really...."

²The Israeli monetary unit is the shekel, which consists of 100 agorot.

"Listen." I turned to Ervinke. "What would have happened if I had said Fourteen?"

"What a question! I'd have lost. Now, that is just the charm of poker: you never know how things will turn out. But if your nerves are not up to a little gambling, perhaps we had better call it off."

Without saying another word, I put down 10 agorot on the table. Ervinke did likewise. I pondered my number carefully and opened with Eighteen.

"Damn!" Ervinke said. "I have only Seventeen!"

I swept the money into my pocket and quietly guffawed. Ervinke had certainly not dreamed that I would master the tricks of Jewish poker so quickly. He had probably counted on my opening with Fifteen or Sixteen, but certainly not with Eighteen. Ervinke, his brow in angry furrows, proposed we double the stakes.

"As you like," I sneered, and could hardly keep back my jubilant laughter. In the meantime a fantastic number had occurred to me: Thirty-five!

"Lead!" said Ervinke.

"Thirty-five!"

"Forty-three!"

With that he pocketed the 40 agorot. I could feel the blood rushing to my brain.

"Listen," I hissed. "Then why didn't you say Forty-three the last time?"

"Because I had thought of Seventeen!" Ervinke retorted indignantly. "Don't you see, that is the fun in poker: you never know what will happen next."

"A shekel," I remarked dryly, and, my lips curled in scorn, I threw a note on the table. Ervinke extracted a similar note from his pocket and with maddening slowness placed it next to mine. The tension was unbearable. I opened with Fifty-four.

"Oh, damn it!" Ervinke fumed. "I also thought of Fifty-four! Draw! Another game!"

My brain worked with lightning speed. "Now you think I'll again call Eleven, my boy," I reasoned. "But you'll get the surprise of your life." I chose the sure-fire Sixty-nine.

"You know what, Ervinke" – I turned to Ervinke – "you lead."

"As you like," he agreed. "It's all the same with me. Seventy!"

Everything went black before my eyes. I had not felt such panic since the siege of Jerusalem.

"*Nu?*" Ervinke urged. "What number did you think of?"

"What do you know?" I whispered with downcast eyes. "I have forgotten."

"You liar!" Ervinke flared. "I know you didn't forget, but simply thought of a smaller number and now you don't want to own up. An old trick. Shame on you!"

I almost slapped his loathsome face for this evil slander, but with some difficulty overcame the urge. With blazing eyes I upped the stakes by another shekel and thought of a murderous number: Ninety-six!

"Lead, stinker," I threw at Ervinke, whereupon he leaned across the table and hissed into my face: "Sixteen hundred and eighty-three!"

A queer weakness gripped me.

"Eighteen hundred," I mumbled wearily.

"Double!" Ervinke shouted, and pocketed the 4 shekels.

"What do you mean, 'double?'" I snorted. "What's that?"

"If you lose your temper in poker, you'll lose your shirt!" Ervinke lectured me. "Any child can understand that my number doubled is higher than yours, so it's clear that. . . ."

"Enough," I hissed and threw down 5 shekels. "Two thousand," I led.

"Two thousand four hundred and seventeen," crowed Ervinke.

"Double!" I sneered, and grabbed the stakes, but Ervinke caught my hand.

"Redouble!" he whispered, and pocketed the 10 shekels. I felt I was going out of my mind.

"Listen" – I gritted my teeth – "if that's how things stand, I could also have said 'redouble' in the last game, couldn't I?"

"Of course," Ervinke agreed. "To tell you the truth, I was rather surprised you didn't. But this is poker, *yahabibi*,³ you either know how to play it or you don't! If you are scatterbrained, better stick to croquet."

The stakes were 10 shekels. "Lead!" I screamed. Ervinke leaned back in his chair, and in a disquietingly calm voice announced his number: Four.

"Ten million!" I blared triumphantly. But without the slightest sign of excitement, Ervinke said: "Ultimo!"

And took the 20 shekels.

I then broke into sobs. Ervinke stroked my hair and told me that according to Hoyle, whoever is first out with the ultimo wins, regardless of numbers. That is the fun in poker: you have to make split-second decisions.

"Twenty shekels," I whimpered, and placed my last notes in the hands of fate. Ervinke also placed his money. My face was bathed in cold sweat. Ervinke went on calmly blowing smoke rings; only his eyes had narrowed.

"Who leads?"

"You," I answered and he fell into my trip like the sucker he was.

"So I lead," Ervinke said. "Ultimo," and he stretched out his hand for the treasure.

"Just a moment" – I stopped him – "Ben-Gurion!"

With that I pocketed the Mint's six-month output. "Ben-Gurion is even stronger than ultimo," I explained. "But it's getting dark outside. Perhaps we had better break it off."

We paid the waiter and left.

Ervinke asked for his money back, saying that I had invented the Ben-Gurion on the spur of the moment. I admitted this, but said that the fun in poker lay in the rule that you never returned money you had won.

---

³Yahabibi – Arab equivalent of "old chap." This address is used only by very intimate friends, or in the street by complete strangers, or schoolchildren at school, or Cabinet Ministers among themselves.

☐ *The parking-place explosion is one of mankind's most acute crises, and, except for the Communist Bloc, no one has succeeded in solving the problem. The situation is becoming more critical day by day: in the United States there are three cars for every fifth person, while in Israel every fifth person is a traffic cop.*

THE ESPRESSO GAMBIT

———□———

We were sitting in our favorite café, Ervinke and me, nursing two espressos and throwing longing glances at the NO PARKING sign outside. In the passage, half-frozen flu germs were coughing spasmodically. Dusk was descending at a slanting angle. Ervinke stirred the opaque liquid absent-mindedly. At this time of the day the car-adoption ritual should be just about to start. But the first cop didn't show up until 10:00 P.M. – a lanky pardner with a rattail mustache and a haughty gait. Ervinke waited until the Law drew up in front of a fire-engine-red sports car and pulled out his wad of tickets; then, with perfect timing, he dashed out of the café.

"Just a sec," Ervinke gasped, "I only went in for a minute . . . just to have an espresso. . . ."

"Sir," said the Law, "tell that to the judge."

"Now really, officer," Ervinke whined, "be a sport. After all, I'm here *now*. . . ."

"Sir, you are interfering with my work!"

"But I only went in for a minute. . . ."

The cop filled out the ticket with sadistic deliberation, then raised a pair of burning eyes. "Look there, sir," he said. "What's written on that sign?"

"Parking forbidden for six meters," Ervinke mumbled contritely. "But just for an espresso, really. . . ."

"Sir," said the cop, "another provocative remark and I'll apply para. seventeen as well, for parking too far from the curb."

"See?" Ervinke snorted. "That's why people hate you!"

" 'Para. seventeen.' " The cop wrote it down evenly and added: "I'm going to run you in, sir!"

"But why?"

"I don't owe you any explanations, sir. Your papers, please!"

Ervinke handed them over.

"Sir," the Law snapped, "I don't need your Sick Fund card! Where is your driving license?"

"I haven't got one."

"You haven't got one? Very well! 'Para. twenty-three!' Have you got a car license, insurance policy?"

"No."

"No?"

"No. Nor have I got a car."

Silence.

Weird, pulsating silence.

"Then," the traffic cop whispered, "then to whom does this red sports car . . . belong?"

"How am I to know?" Ervinke shot back. "I only went in for a quick espresso. That's what I've been trying to tell you all along, but you didn't give me a chance."

The cop blanched, turned into antimatter, his jaws moving rhythmically. His expression will haunt me for many sleepless nights. Purple-faced, he stuck the ticket on the sports car's windshield and left. At the corner he disintegrated with a sharp report.

Altogether, it had been a pleasant, entertaining evening.

CASTOR OIL DAY

Some days ago, I was sitting with Ervinke in a café bitterly bemoaning the moral morass into which our poor country had sunk: the cafés are full of well-to-do drones living on Heaven knows what. For three mornings we had sat there trying to solve the mystery but couldn't. At the same time here are we, two mature young men ready to conquer the desert – and having to make ends meet on a ridiculously low salary. Why, we asked ourselves, why? Then we rose, paid, and prepared to move on to another café, when Ervinke suddenly saw a small brown package lying on a chair next to his. It had been lying there for quite a long time, but we had not seen it.

"Hey," I said to Ervinke, "we ought to give it to the headwaiter."

"Of course," Ervinke answered vaguely. "But must it be right away?"

In short, we fought a losing battle against our consciences, until Ervinke in the end hit upon the right solution.

"We'll open the parcel before we hand it over," he said. "Who knows, perhaps there is a wad of faked dollars in it and we might get into trouble if we return it."

I bowed to this argument. We tore the brown paper and found inside about a hundred thousand small labels of the kind one sticks on medicine bottles:

OL. RICINI

CASTOR OIL

Shake well before using

When Ervinke saw the labels, he turned deathly pale and

stuttered, trembling with excitement, "My God, a fortune has fallen into our hands. We are rich."

At first I thought the overdose of coffee had driven Ervinke out of his mind and tried to calm him. Ervinke paid no heed to my soothing words but ran out of the café into the nearest ironmonger's, dragging me along. He bought two pounds of pins.

After that we got cracking.

Ervinke stopped the first middle-aged gentleman who came our way and pinned a label on his lapel.

"How much?" the gentleman asked.

"As you like," Ervinke said and got 50 agorot. Then came a lady with two little girls. Ervinke pinned a label on her, whereupon the little girls started bawling "Mommy, me too!" We got another 50 agorot. A well-dressed man gave us 1 shekel but haughtily stuffed the castor oil ticket into his pocket. The average donation was 50 agorot. A young existentialist protested against the pinning, saying he was not religious. And another man said he would be "damned if I'll contribute to that fascist fund of yours."

Later we split our stock and started working separately. Within less than three hours, some passersby were actually pointing to their lapels as proof that they had already donated to our charity.

By noon we had run out of pins and bought another two pounds. By nightfall there was nobody in the city without castor oil on his lapel. We had disposed of our whole supply. I had made about 10,000 shekels while Ervinke, who was quicker with the pins, had made 14,000.

Tomorrow: Haifa. The day after tomorrow: Jerusalem.

Beware the Guard

———□———

One hot evening we decided, Ervinke and I, to have a look at that much-vaunted Home and Garden Exhibition said to be such a favorite with young and pretty housewives. So we jumped into my car and dashed down to the grounds. I parked on the square in front of the gate and went to buy tickets, while Ervinke leaned against the wall and picked his teeth.

Suddenly a gentleman came up to him and asked, "How much?"

"Thirty-five agorot," Ervinke said, and took the money. But the gentleman did not go away and seemed to be waiting for something. In the end he asked, "Don't you give me a slip of paper?"

"What slip of paper?"

"What do you mean what slip of paper? For my car."

"Oh, that!" Ervinke replied, took out his notebook, tore out a leaf from it and wrote down the number of the gentleman's car: "T 14948."

The gentleman carefully folded the slip of paper and stowed it away in his billfold. He just wanted to know why he had to pay 35 agorot when in front of the swimming pool they took only 20 agorot for guarding a car?

Ervinke replied that he took 35 agorot, and if the gentleman did not like it, he could park his car in front of the swimming pool.

The gentleman went into the exhibition, his face crimson, while Ervinke stayed on, pondering the possibilities inherent in the situation.

From then on Ervinke did not wait for the customers to come to him, but whenever a car or motorcycle pulled up, he would hail the man sitting at the wheel, give him a slip of paper on which he had written the number of the vehicle and the exact date, and say, "Thirty-five agorot."

Only one driver, a notorious miser, refused to pay, backed out, and parked his car three kilometers from the gate (just to save 35 agorot!). Within ten minutes we had run out of notebook leaves, so I had to tear up a Last Warning from the Execution Office, which I happened to have on me, and on these slips of paper Ervinke wrote down the numbers and dates.

When the Last Warning fragments had gone, we went into the exhibition and had a friendly chat with the demonstrator of an automatic potato-peeling machine. She wanted to give us her phone number, but we could not find even a piece of confetti to write it on.

By the time we left the exhibition, we had practically forgotten the cars entrusted to our care, when suddenly our first customer popped out of the darkness, scared to death, and waved his slip of paper in our faces. It seemed that somebody had stolen his car. Ervinke checked the paper closely and said, "T 14948. The gentleman is right. Here are your thirty-five agorot."

Ervinke paid him in cash and we flew to Cyprus for the weekend.

CHOP STORY

We were sitting on top of Mt. Carmel nursing our instants and surveying the clean pavements and well-mannered population of Haifa outside. A lone fly crawled over our table but didn't dare buzz aloud. The air was heavy, but still. Ervinke was sitting chin in hand over a pile of magazines and tsk-tsking at the slander columns.

"Extortion has its point," my friend remarked at last. "Shall we?"

I paid and we left. Our first butcher shop was right across the street from the café. Ervinke unbuttoned his shirt halfway down his chest and we went in.

"Morning," Ervinke announced. "We are the new racket."

The butcher looked puzzled:

"Why?" he asked. "What happened?"

"They quit," Ervinke explained, "and we are taking over. Did you use to pay monthly or by the truckload?"

"By the load."

"Then from now on you'll pay monthly. Three thousand each first of the month."

"Three thousand?"

"That's the charge. Any idea how much it costs to maintain a mafia these days?"

"Sorry," the butcher said doggedly, "I only paid half that much before."

"That's what old Schlesinger said too, may his soul rest in peace," mumbled Ervinke and thrust his hand casually into his right trouser pocket. The butcher stepped back against the counter with blazing eyes: "I ... I...." he stuttered, "I'll complain to the Marketing Board!"

"Wise up!" Ervinke smiled. "That's where we're from."

"I'll complain to the Council!"

"Like Lewinsohn did last Tuesday?" asked Ervinke with a slight frown. "You looking for trouble?"

"I'm a Labor Union member!"

"Aren't we all?" said Ervinke. "So?"

"I'll truck the meat myself," growled the man. "I shall fight for my rights from inside the Party!"

"Poofff!" Ervinke spluttered with laughter. "The Party . . . that's a good one. . . ."

He barely managed to calm down.

"Listen, Butch," he said amiably at last, "have you forgotten what happened to poor old Mittagessen?"

"I'll call the Police!"

"I can spare you the trouble," said Ervinke, cleaning his nails. "I'm having lunch with the Chief Inspector at two."

"I'll inform the Mayor!"

"Ooh! Now you've really got me scared."

"I'll go as high as the Minister!"

"I'll come along."

"Ai!" groaned the butcher, "God in heaven!"

"He knows all about it."

The butcher burst out sobbing. Ervinke stroked his head: "We realize it's tough," he said gently, "but such is life, Butchie. Expenses keep mounting. Not so long ago you could get a fairly decent submachine gun for five thousand shekels. Today it's twice that. And bribes? Only last year a senior official cost two thousand, now they're asking six, eight thousand net! A judge is twelve thousand! What can we do?"

In the end we agreed on two instalments, one down and the other on the last of the month. In exchange, Butch acquired the right to transport his own meat in his own truck to his own shop. The man hardly knew how to thank us. He was a nice guy, really. A bit highly strung, that's all. He sent us off with a dozen lamb chops and a turkey. Eventually they learn what's due.

☐ *Whatever one may say of Israel, it has terrific sex appeal. Otherwise one could not explain its dizzying success with tourists. Sex appeal — that's what we have. Especially in our famous spa, Eilat, where the tourist miracle takes on Biblical proportions.*

A Seaful of Miracles

We have been in Eilat only once, quite a long time ago. Although our stay was brief, we exhausted practically all the rich opportunities for entertainment offered by this unforgettable place. We visited King Solomon's pillars, splashed in the Red Sea, took a brief nap, then, greatly refreshed, dashed down to Solomon's columns, inspected the columns, swam a few strokes and squeezed in a trip to the columns.

But all this is not a patch on that great international attraction, the glass-bottomed boat. That world-famous frigate enables you to view in comfort all the wonders of the deep blue.

It is related that quite a few tourists have come down to Eilat planning to stay a day, rashly boarded the boat and are now incurably addicted to it.

Small wonder then if we also succumbed to the lure and bought a ride on it. Our fellow travellers were a Canadian millionaire with his wife and a couple of lovers. The navigation company provided the appropriate romantic atmosphere. The seats had been left in the innocent, rough-hewn state, and the glass bottom had not been scrubbed for ages. The captain was an old sea dog.

We put to sea without a hitch. As if a magic wand had been passed over it, the bottom suddenly spread out under us, flat, without a ripple, with each grain of sand scintillating in the green opaqueness of the sea.

For about thirty minutes we drifted over it, and the wonderful sand never once changed its texture. Never before had we seen sand so faultless, so uniform, so devoid of discordant features, only smooth sand, continuous sand, exclusively sand. Grunting ecstatically, the Canadian millionaire took pictures.

"There!" the millionairess shouted and pointed a shaking finger downward. "There!"

We looked down and our hearts almost stopped beating. On the undulating bottom, in the blinking twilight, we made out a dark form partially covered with seaweed. No doubt about it; it was a huge bus tire spreading a mysterious calm all around it.

We continued our dream-like trip. The young couple pointed, giggling, at the yellow-tinted rocks gliding by underneath. The Canadian remarked that he had seen many rocks in a life of globe-trotting, but never such uniform ones as these.

Strewn among the rocks were all the treasures of the Arabian Nights: a wide assortment of bottles, empty and full, round and square, broken and whole, some of them filled with colored sand of the kind sold to shore-bound tourists.

It was as if Jules Verne's fabulous story-worlds had come alive before our amazed eyes. We practically stopped breathing with the excitement of it all. Unexpectedly, something moved.

"Fish!" I screamed. "Fish!"

The old man of the sea again cut the engine, so that we might better enjoy the unforgettable sight.

Practically under our feet, three sardines flashed by in a flurry of glittering fins, then disappeared among the cracks.

The old seaman announced, "Gentlemen, there is a sunken ship right under us."

We bowed deeply over the glass bottom, afraid to miss anything of the majestic sight. At first we could not make out anything in the murk, but slowly our eyes became accustomed to it and we saw that we could really not distinguish anything at all.

"The sand has covered it completely," the sea dog explained in a choked voice, and in our mind's eye we saw the frightful tragedy taking its inexorable course in the depths of the cruel sea. The young lady began to tremble and begged to be taken back.

"All right," the millionaire agreed, "but I must see the Kent once more!"

The captain veered to starboard at a sharp angle and set out for the open sea at full throttle. After a mad chase of about half a minute, we stopped. The millionaire dropped flat on his face and shouted rapturously, "Kent! Kent!"

At the foot of a rock there appeared a virginally white and whole cigarette carton. Only one side of it had been opened. The inscription was still legible; only the "nt" had become covered with some kind of fungus. The millionaire took a few low-angle shots of the carton, then we returned to base.

If I forget thee, O, Eilat, may my right hand lose its cunning.

◻ *If a rich Jew wants to help Israel, he builds a hotel in it. Which, by the way, is also a good business proposition: the suckers from abroad are just begging to be skinned. But woe to the Israeli who takes a room there!*

I myself once made this costly error. Somehow I had managed to save a few shekels from the clutches of the taxman, and decided to spend a pleasant vacation at one of these super de luxe hotels. I chose one that boasts a golf course, a cricket pitch, and a poker lounge, to say nothing of a special race track (Wednesday nights).

Now It Can Be Told

My taxi pulled up at the main entrance, and an aide in a dazzling uniform grabbed my suitcase and said: "Room number, sir?"

"Don't know," I replied. "I've just arrived."

He bowed me toward the marble-bedecked reception desk, where a secret service man disclosed my room number: 157. Hearing this, the aide pulled out a notebook from his pocket and wrote in it "157." I shrugged this off as just another manifestation of legendary Germanic orderliness. The secret service presented me with a diamond-studded 24-carat gold key, I walked up to my room, whose number was 157, opened the cupboards, and unpacked. When I wanted to wash my hands, I found that there was no soap. I rang for one of the slave girls, who brought me a brand-new Hollywood soap marvel and asked: "Room number, please?"

"One fifty-seven," I replied enthusiastically. The slave girl took out a notebook and wrote in it "157." I raised an eyebrow, then stepped down to the restaurant. They gave me two slices of toast with my tea. The toast was absolutely divine, so I asked for another slice.

"Room number?" the ramrod-stiff ex-diplomat waiter asked. The "157" was duly noted. Afterward I went back to my room to change into a dinner jacket, and on the way asked the time from one of the brigadiers employed as porters.

"My room number is one fifty-seven," I said to the brigadier. "What's the time?"

"Five-thirty," the porter answered, and wrote "157" in a thick ledger. Later I asked for a clothesbrush (157) and that my room be sprayed with DDT (157). All this bookkeeping made me slightly nervous, so I turned up before the hotel manager's boudoir and applied for a special audience.

"Why do I always have to mention my room number, my lord?" I asked.

His lordship rested a disapproving glance on my tiresome person, then coolly replied: "Every service not included in the full board," he explained in his cultured Oxonian voice,[1] "is added to the guest's bill. That is why the staff asks for the number of your room, sir. What is your room number, sir?"

"One fifty-seven."

"Thank you, sir," said his lordship as he wrote on a slip of paper "Inform. No. 157."

From then on, "157" became my life's leitmotiv. Two days later I no longer dared address the staff without mentioning the "157." And once, when I asked for grapefruit juice and there was none, I called the waiter's attention to the fact that he should have written "No grpfrt. for 157."

Four days later, it got so that I introduced myself jailbird fashion: "One fifty-seven. Pleased to meet you."

"Very pleased indeed," Prince Weingartner, the hotel secretary, at once replied, and wrote in his notebook "Introduced self to No. 157."

Quite unexpectedly, my whole outlook was changed. I was sitting on the hotel's amethyst veranda, deeply breathing the ozone-

---

[1] Only Oxford English is spoken in these hotels, so that American Jews have to employ an interpreter to make themselves understood. But if worse comes to worst, they can always fall back on Yiddish.

laden evening air, when one of the overseers stepped up to me, drawn notebook in hand.

"One fifty-seven," I said politely. "For air."

"Fifty-seven," the overseer wrote. "Thank you, sir."

I was on the point of setting him right, but a mysterious inner force held me back. Certain bizarre thoughts began chasing around in my brain. They all concerned certain rather obvious possibilities inherent in the situation. I sat down in the restaurant and ordered an extra-large extracurricular portion of grilled liver.

"Room number?" the waiter, a retired colonel of the Guards, asked.

"Seventy-five," I answered.

"75," the colonel (ret.) wrote. "Thank you, sir."

That's how it started. During the next few days I realized several ambitions that until now had seemed too fantastic for serious consideration. Twice I ordered luxury yachts (75), three times belly dancers (75) and once performing midgets (75). Nothing was too good for me, because it is my firm conviction that at least on vacations one should not be stingy. If you cannot think of anything but the cost, better stay home and buy yourself an orange grove.

The day before yesterday, after spending a wonderful fortnight, I left the hotel. Prince Weingartner presented me with the bill, hand-signed by His Lordship the Manager. I paid 390 shekels, which included such special services as soap (5 shekels), information (3 shekels 10 agorot), evening breather (4 shekels 90 agorot), and a few other trifles. With a manly handshake, I took leave of the staff, gave the brigadier 100 shekels, his aide only 50 shekels.[2]

As I marched toward the taxi in the wake of my suitcase, a stubby and balding gentleman was throwing a fit at the reception desk. He tore his bill to shreds, babbling some incoherent nonsense about

---

[2] Generally you don't tip in Israel, because that, according to the guests, is contrary to human dignity as defined in the United Nations charter. The waiters' outlook is less dogmatic.

refusing to pay 2,600 shekels as he had not ordered twenty-nine portions of grilled liver. Is there really no other way of settling one's differences in this country than by shouting?

☐ *Every citizen departing the country causes us a great deal of heartbreak, but if a football player leaves just because he is offered a measly few thousand dollars, that is a national disaster. Our sports authorities are doing everything in their power to stop the mass flight, and are offering fabulous sums to everybody involved, except to the players themselves, because that would qualify as appeasement.*

THE GREAT FLIGHT

"Is Pommie going to play?"

Yes, that was the question which on that Sabbath afternoon worried the fans of the champion team Lightning-Holon, due to meet Hapoel Kfar Maccabi in a fateful match of the National League. The excitement was understandable: according to well-informed circles, the team's coach had been given secret orders by the management to keep an eye on the players, and the spectators indeed saw him before the start of the game, running about among the players, counting them and double-checking.

The reason was well known to all: the team scouts had found passports in the effects of several players, among them the legendary Pommie, as the affectionate fans had nicknamed Pomerantz. As a matter of fact, this surprised only those who did not know the real Pommie. This football star extorted from his club everything that could be extorted. Not only had they arranged light work for him – part-time baby-sitting with a childless family – but on top of that they had granted him an increased training bonus as well as overtime. Everybody thought that Pomerantz was at last satisfied, but about two weeks earlier the player had been seen leaving a bookstore carrying – an English dictionary!

The club had acted promptly: two full-time detectives were hired and assigned to tail Pommie wherever he went. The open clash between Pommie and his club happened on the Wednesday, when the player came to the manager and demanded that he, too, be hired as a detective.

"I can tail myself better than anyone else," Pommie explained, "and then at least I'll be able to live on my salary."

"Never!" the manager answered, the veins bulging in his neck. "I won't tolerate professionalism here! We won't sink into the shameful quagmire in which English, Hungarian and Brazilian football has been for many years now. You are a sportsman, Pomerantz!"

"All right, so from now on I want to be considered an entertainer."

"Never," said the manager. "You shouldn't make your living out of football!"

"Then call it footballet!"

"Never!" The manager raised his voice. "As long as I manage the club at the head of which my party has placed me, I shall not permit ugly professionalism. Because," the manager added, "if they should introduce ugly professionalism, I won't be able to keep my job at the head of the club. Is that clear?"

That sounded logical. Pomerantz left without another word and on that very day ostentatiously bought himself particularly dark sunglasses, as the detectives pointed out in their daily report. The alarming signs quickly multiplied: suddenly the player's wife appeared to be calm and happy, she dyed her hair blond, then . . . she bought . . . two suitcases!

The entire Football Federation was gripped by panic.

"The situation is serious," the Secretary General frankly admitted to the assembled Executive. "A star player like Pomerantz nets our Federation about a million shekels a year, and yet the bastard is now plotting to flee abroad because they are offering him Sh.600 a month. What can we do to prevent him from leaving? For goodness sake, what is to be done? What can we do?"

It was indeed a hard question. The Football Federation had

· THE GREAT FLIGHT ·

already tried everything to instill some order into this important branch of sport. After losing against Luxembourg (1:14), revolutionary changes were introduced in the Federation's set up: Hapoel received twelve seats on the Executive – i.e. an additional representative at the expense of Maccabi – and another floor was added to the office building at a cost of half a million shekels. It was then that two fullbacks, a halfback and a slightly used left-wing deserted the National Team and emigrated to Australia, South Africa and Ghana respectively. The Federation reacted promptly. The salary of the National Team coach, Hodja Czorjekracj from Albania, was raised to Sh. 2,000 a week and the number of officials was doubled.

Even this did not help.

What was to be done? What could be done to keep the players?

Lightning-Holon made a last desperate effort which bordered on humiliation: the team manager took Pomerantz down to the Negev, and in the middle of the wilderness, out of range of any human ear, he made him a whispered offer of a Sh. 3 premium for every goal scored by him.

"Score a hundred goals a month," the manager proposed, "and you've got three hundred net, tax free."

Seeing the player's blank face, the manager proposed to pay Sh. 1.50 even for a successful penalty kick. But Pommie stood there, pale and adamant.

"Four hundred," he said. "Fixed salary!"

Without loss of time, the watch on Pomerantz was reinforced by four additional detectives. The deployment of this huge apparatus for preventing escapes was a great burden on the Federation's budget, but that venerable institution was ready to make any sacrifice for the sake of a healthy sports life. And it must be admitted that it was only thanks to these special precautions that Pommie showed up against Hapoel Kfar Maccabi on that fateful day.

The detective groups' actions were fully coordinated. The two tailing scouts reported by radio during the early morning hours that Mrs. Pomerantz had left the house carrying a suitcase. Within twenty minutes the Lydda Airport group discovered that a seat had been booked for a mystery passenger with a cargo of balls on the plane to Rome. What happened then is known from the daily press: the plane was confiscated. The frontiers were closed. At 1:00 P.M. the player left his home and jumped into a taxi, where two strong-arm boys were waiting for him. They hit him over the head with rubber truncheons.

Pommie regained consciousness at the football field, in his team's locker room. The coach faced him, a cocked pistol in his hand.

"You make just one suspicious move and I'll shoot you down like a mad dog," the coach said. "Now get out and play!"

Pomerantz offered only token resistance. "Come on, be a sport, pay me at least a Sh.7 obedience premium."

"Out!"

Pommie doubled out of the locker room with the rest of the team. The eyes of fifty thousand fans were on him. They had paid Sh.10 per head to see him. By then everybody knew that the Federation had asked for an injunction to prevent Pommie's leaving the country, since this represented a *de facto* smuggling of capital abroad.

The rest is known to every family in Israel from the mouth of the popular sportscaster:

" . . . the ball is with Pomerantz in this nineteenth minute of the game," the favorite sportscaster reported. "He passes with a marvelous feint the player appointed to guard him, runs at full speed the length of the touchline, does some brilliant dribbling and drops the two fullbacks, turns right, passes the goal line still carrying the ball, runs up the stairs of the grandstand, dodges three spectators who try to stop him, dashes past the coach, climbs the fence and jumps clear of the field – in the twenty-first minute Pomerantz has escaped!"

The audience rose to its feet, thrilled by the superb performance, but soon enough it was discovered that Pommie had been stopped outside. The management of Lightning-Holon had bagged him in a net spread out below the fence. The ball again passed into the hands of the Federation.

"Pommie, don't be a fool," the club chairman gasped as he

dragged the center forward back into the stadium. "We'll give you a Sh.5.50 haircut premium and a cheese sandwich before every game."

Complete anarchy reigned on the field. The goalkeeper of Hapoel Kfar Maccabi had taken advantage of the disturbance created by Pomerantz's break and tried to escape through the police gate. At the last minute he was returned in handcuffs and his club chairman tried to appease him with a one-time stay-put premium. The referee noticed what was happening and ruled a penalty shot for a violation of amateurship.

Who would kick the penalty shot?

Pommie! Pommie!

Pomerantz prepared carefully, took off and landed a mighty kick – in the ground. The ball did not even reach the goal.

What had happened? the audience wondered. This was not their Pommie! This was somebody else!

And, indeed, only then was it noticed that the player down there was short, thin and hirsute, whereas Pommie was a bald giant.

This happened in the thirty-eighth minute!

The real Pomerantz had left the country ten minutes earlier in a small motorboat headed in the general direction of Cyprus. The operation had been planned with an eye for detail worthy of *Rififi*. Pommie had indeed climbed the fence, but somebody else disguised as Pomerantz had jumped off it. The time he gained had enabled him to make the seashore. The plane ticket had been a decoy. The suitcase had been filled with stones. He was not even married. Today Pommie is the star of the Skymaster team in Zimbabwe, he makes $5,000 a month net, and has a lot of chestnut-haired servant girls. And what's even more annoying, he is the co-author of the bestseller *I Was Pomerantz's Double*.

☐ *Ever since delivery from Egyptian bondage, the Jewish people have been considered the unflinching champions of freedom. More than that, we were the first to legislate the liberation of slaves, in all sorts of revolutions we carried high the banner of equality between man and man, and now in our young fatherland we have at long last freed from its bonds the Jewish washing machine as well.*

Born to Be Free

———◻———

One evening not long ago, the wife informed me that we needed a new washing machine, since the old one was overtaxed by our country's climatic conditions. What the little one meant was that in winter we expected an extra effort from the washing machine since it has to launder every single piece of underwear at least three times because of the rain maliciously wetting what is hung outdoors to dry. In view of the particularly rainy season, there was no doubt at all that we needed a younger and more virile machine.

"All right," I gave the little one the green light, "go and buy a washing machine, but just one and as locally manufactured as you can find."

She is very good at buying, the little one. The very next day a Hebrew washing machine with highly polished knobs, a long cord and instructions was humming pleasantly on our paved kitchen patio. It was love at first wash, as the ads say. It did all the washing automatically from soaping to wringing, as if endowed with human intelligence.

And that is exactly what the story is about.

At noon on that Tuesday the wife came into my study and said, somewhat upset: "Ephraim! Our machine is walking!"

I followed her at the double to the kitchen patio and there beheld the contraption engaged in "spin drying" and at the same time moving with remarkable hops toward the kitchen. We stopped it literally on the threshold by pressing the red panic button, and sized up the situation. We found that it walked only while spin drying, as then the drum spun at a dizzying speed, the body of the contraption started vibrating terribly and – hop! hop! hop! – it was impelled forward by an uncontrollable inner urge.

We did not attach too much importance to this phenomenon. After all, our home is not a prison and if the machine felt like taking a spin on the patio, that's O.K. with us.

One stormy night we were awakened by the scrunch of tortured metal coming from the patio and, going out there, we found Amir's tricycle completely smashed, lying under our spin-drying machine. The kid howled at the top of his voice and beat his little fists against the sides of the wayward appliance: "Phooey, naughty laundry, phooey!"

"I won't take any chances," the woman decided, "I'll tie Jonathan up!"

She took a piece of rope and tied the appliance to the hot-water tap. I didn't feel too good about this, but did not intervene – after all, it was her machine and thus she had the right to tie it up if she felt like it. But I can't, nor do I want to, deny that next morning I felt most sympathetic when we found Jonathan on the other side of the patio. He had put his horsepowers to work and snapped the rope. The woman gritted her teeth and tied it up again, this time to the gas tanks.

The ear-splitting racket sparked off by this act will forever linger in my memory.

"Ephraim," the woman whispered, "it's dragging the gas tanks along."

The copper pipe was bent to breaking point and there was a penetrating smell of cooking gas in the air. We realized it would not be wise to tie up Jonathan again since he obviously resented it. After this incident we left him to his laundering in complete freedom. Somehow we got used to the idea that our washing machine was a noble Israeli animal which would not tolerate any kind of rein. Only once, on a

Saturday night, it caused an unpleasant incident when it burst into the dining room and started annoying our guests.

"Out," the wife screamed, "get out! Back to your kennel!"

As if a washing machine could understand what one is saying to it! I pressed the red button and stopped it dead in its tracks. When the guests had left I restarted Jonathan so as to lead him back, but it seems that he was past the spin dry stage and, as will be remembered, this was his only ambulatory stage. We had to go through the whole process again, a lengthy operation.

In the meantime Amir had made great friends with the machine. He rode all day long on Jonathan, shouting: "Giddy-up, giddy-up!"

Very nice. Jonathan also launders extremely well, goes easy on the washing powder. Indeed, except for his penchant toward side trips, we have no complaints against him. However, on one of those murky afternoons he gave me a bad scare. I came home through the garage and there was spinning Jonathan coming toward me in huge jumps. If I had been just a few minutes later he would have reached the road through the open garage door.

"Say," the wife mused, her eyes dreaming. "Couldn't we send him to do the shopping at the supermarket?"

There was nothing we could do but consult a specialist. With a heavy heart I went to see the representative of the factory and told him our tale of woe. The specialist was not a bit surprised.

"Yes, yes," he agreed. "They run when they spin. But only if you put too little laundy in the drum. In that case a centrifugal imbalance is created which pushes the machine forward. Fill Jonathan up with at least four kilos of laundry and he won't budge, I promise."

I came back from the specialist filled with satisfaction and joy. I found the little one weeding in the garden. I told her that for lack of enough dirty linen our machine was running centrifugally amok.

The wife blanched. "Good Lord," she stuttered, "today I put just two kilos in it."

We hurried to the patio and the world went black before our

eyes. Jonathan had disappeared. Shouting hoarsely, I burst into the road.

"Jonathan! Jonathan!"

I sped along the houses and asked the neighbors whether they had seen a Hebrew-speaking washing machine walking toward the city. The neighbors shook their heads regretfully. One of them asked what color the machine was; another remarked that he seemed to remember seeing something like that in front of the post office, but we found that it was a refrigerator some porters had carelessly left there.

After a long and fruitless search I returned home utterly dejected. Who knows, perhaps in the meantime a bus had run down the poor kid – those drivers are all maniacs. Tears were in my eyes. Our Jonathan, freedom-loving son of our industrial jungle, was now facing all the dangers of the big city's wild traffic. Should his "spin dry" stop in the middle of the road, he would no longer be able to move . . . and would stand there . . . in the middle of Allenby Road. . . .

"He's here!" The little one came running toward me. "He's here!"

What had happened was that while the wife was innocently weeding the garden, the little idiot had stepped into the hallway, skipped toward the basement steps and had been stopped at the very last moment when he inadvertently pulled the plug out from the wall, a deed which saved him from a certain crash.

"Enough!" the wife decided. "Take off your underwear!"

And since then she has been collecting all the potential laundry to be found in our house, stuffing Jonathan with four and a half kilos of washing. And indeed, since then Jonathan has not budged an inch. It's all he can do to breathe and turn the top-heavy drum within his belly.

"Poor fellow," I mumbled seeing him so brutally immobilized, "it's a shame to do this to him."

Yesterday something snapped within me. I quietly stopped him at "spin" and removed at least a kilo and a half. Jonathan again started frolicking gaily and made a beeline for the pretty Italian washing machine across the street, sounding a happy masculine rumble – just like old times.

I patted his trembling flanks. "Go, Jonathan, go!"

He was born to be free.

☐ *Somehow or other, one can cope with a frolicsome washing machine, because its vocabulary is somewhat limited. But the situation becomes critical if one has to face a computer of Jewish origin. To the best of our knowledge, the monster computer of the Ministry of Finance in Jerusalem is the only one in the world that ever notified its superiors: "Gentlemen, yesterday afternoon I went out of my mind, over."*

THE JERUSALEM GOLEM

———☐———

One evening not long ago I received a note from the State of Israel Revenue Department. It was only an official slip of paper written in shaky print, saying: "Last warning before seizure. Since you have not acted on our notifications regarding your debt to the amount of Sh.20,012.11 in payment of repairs carried out in the Kishon River Harbor in July 1961, may I draw your attention to the fact that unless you pay the above debt within seven days we shall apply to you the provisions of the law regarding the seizure of your property and its sale." Such were the words of the Revenue Department, somewhat tempered by the last paragraph: "If in the meantime you have settled your debt, please disregard this notification." Signed: "S. Seligson, Department Head."

Slight panic seized me upon receiving this letter.

On the one hand, a careful examination of my books proved beyond the shadow of a doubt that no repair work had been carried out on me lately, but on the other hand I could not claim by any stretch of the imagination that I had settled the above matter with the authorities in the words of the warning. And since I am for the settlement of local conflicts by direct negotiation, I went to the Revenue Department and had a personal talk with Mr. Seligson.

"Here," I said, showing him my identity card. "I am a writer and not a river."

The Department Head looked at me closely. "Then why are you called Kishon?"

"It's a habit," I set things right. "But I'm also Ephraim, and the river isn't."

That did it. The Head apologized and went to the next room in order to discuss the painful matter with his associates. They conferred in hushed tones, looked in from time to time, and once asked me to turn around with raised hands. In the end they were convinced of the validity of my case, or at least gave me the benefit of the doubt. The Head of the Department, Seligson, came back and canceled the warning, writing on my file in red pencil: "He has no harbor! Seligson." He also drew a big zero on the file and crossed it through with a diagonal line. I returned to my family greatly relieved.

"It was an error," I informed the wife. "Sheer logic won the day."

"You see," the woman replied. "One shouldn't lose heart straight away."

The Note on the Seizure of Chattels arrived on Wednesday noon. "Since you did not act on the Warning Before Seizure of Chattels and did not pay your debt to the amount of Sh.20,012.11," Mr. Seligson wrote me in the same shaky print, "I shall be forced to apply the provisions of the law regarding the seizure of chattels in your house and business. If in the meantime you have settled your debt, consider this note as canceled."

I went to the Department on the double.

"Yes, yes," Mr. Seligson tried to calm me. "These notes are sent out by the electronic computer in Jerusalem and not by me. It keeps doing this sort of thing, don't worry about it."

It seems that the computer center in Jerusalem introduced automation about a half a year ago, in the spirit of the twentieth century, and since then the computer has been doing the job of ten thousand sad-eyed clerks. The computer's only shortcoming is that the local technicians don't yet know exactly how it works and occasionally feed it data which give it indigestion, as in the case of the harbor repairs. Mr. Seligson promised me that this time the delicate matter would be settled once and for all, and just to be on the safe side, he sent a teleprinter message to Jerusalem: until further notice the handling of my debt should be deferred, on his responsibility. I thanked him for the noble gesture, and returned to my family in excellent spirits.

On Sunday morning they took away the refrigerator. Three brawny Government porters produced an order signed by S. Seligson and then seized my refrigerator and moved it through the door and into the street. I hopped and skipped around them like a startled rooster.

"Am I a river?" I crowed. "Where am I a river? Can a river talk? Can a river jump around?"

Actually, the men were only doing their job. I found Mr. Seligson at the office in utterly dejected mood. Early in the morning a note had reached him from Jerusalem, a first warning about his debt to the amount of Sh.20,012.11 for repairs on me.

"It seems," he told me, his eyes reproachful, "that the computer interpreted the words 'on my responsibility' in this way. One has to be very careful. You put me in a nice fix, my dear sir, I must say!"

I told him that he should regard the note as canceled, but the man was completely hysterical.

"Once the computer gets hold of you, there's nothing you can do about it!" He tore his hair. "Only two months ago the head of the Execution Department received an order from the Jerusalem computer to execute his deputy. Only the Minister's personal intervention saved the fellow at the last minute. His head was literally taken out of the noose."

I proposed that we take a taxi, go up to Jerusalem and have a man-to-man talk with the machine. "Sir," we'd say to it, "kindly recheck your data!"

"You can't talk to it," said Seligson. "It's the busiest computer in the area – they use it for forecasting the weather and interpreting dreams as well."

Just the same, he rang the storeroom of the Jaffa Department and gave orders to defer the sale of my refrigerator until further notice. The refrigerator was sold the same evening at a public auction for Sh.19 in cash, as transpired from the Statement of Debt which reached my house next morning in a most unbureaucratic way. My debt had shrunk to Sh.19,993.11, which must be settled within seven days. If in the meantime. . . .

I waited over an hour for Seligson to come to his office. He had been rushing all over town with his lawyer, had registered his refrigerator in his wife's name, and swore that if ever he got out of the computer's clutches he would never again intervene on anyone's behalf. I asked him what was going to happen to me now.

"I don't know," Seligson answered, breathing heavily. "Sometimes it happens that the computer forgets somebody for months on end, so let's hope. . . ."

I told him that I couldn't trust in miracles, I believed in more concrete things; I wanted to settle the affair once and for all. "As you like," Seligson said, "you have every right." After a brief but stormy argument, we reached an agreement according to which I would pay for the repair of my harbor in twelve monthly instalments. I signed the undertaking and we sent notification of this to Jerusalem in order to save what could still be saved of my chattels.

"This is the best I can do," Seligson apologized. "I'm convinced that in two or three years' time the computer team will get more proficient, but meanwhile I'm sorry."

"Never mind," I consoled him. "One can't have everything at once."

The first check in the amount of Sh.1,666.05 reached me yesterday. Together with the Treasury's check there also arrived Seligson's note, written in the computer's shaky print to the effect that this was the first payment for the Sh.19,993.11 with which I was credited in Jerusalem on March 1, 1969. I remarked to the wife that from now on we had no worries in life, whereupon she remarked that it was a shame they didn't pay us interest as well; one gets 6 percent everywhere else.

"Darling," I said to her, "I am sick and tired of the whole matter,

I'm not going to move another finger."

The future belongs to automation. Please consider this story as canceled.

☐ *Maybe we still have not caught up with the finesses of world power politics, but we did catch up with our people's chief exterminator. His testimony in court illustrated the thought process of a surrealist rat.*

2 × 2 = SCHULTZ: FRAGMENT FROM AN AVANT-GARDE PLAY

Scene: an imaginary courtroom

PROSECUTOR: What's your opinion on twice two?

ADOLF: I'm not a mathematician, sir.

PROSECUTOR: All the same, how much, in your opinion, is twice two?

ADOLF: I have never in my life made such calculations. If I ever ran into such a problem, I referred it to the appropriate department. Decisions, in any case, were always taken by Schultz.

PROSECUTOR: So you don't know how much twice two makes?

ADOLF: I have no authority to say, sir.

PROSECUTOR: And if I tell you that you do know how much is twice two?

ADOLF: Only Schultz dealt with numbers.

PROSECUTOR: So whenever you wanted to know how much twice two was, you went to Schultz?

ADOLF: Not always. Sometimes these things could be arranged by phone. Though may I say that late in 1943 Schultz was moved to the Salzkammergut and it was only there that I met him with Lopke.

PROSECUTOR: Did Lopke also know the answer to twice two?

ADOLF: I don't know. I never asked him. As I said, my superior was Schultz.
PROSECUTOR: Did Schultz know the correct answer to twice two?
ADOLF: I can't know that because I wasn't in his skin.
PROSECUTOR: But it may be presumed that he knew, didn't he?
ADOLF: I never attempted to judge my superiors.
PROSECUTOR: So how did you know that Schultz's calculations with respect to twice two were correct?
ADOLF: I didn't know. If memory serves me, I even entertained some doubts. I'm not a mathematician.
PROSECUTOR: Aren't you? Then perhaps you can tell us how it is possible that Document No. 6013 is annotated in your own handwriting, "twice two is four."
ADOLF: That's impossible.
PROSECUTOR: Here! (*Hands him a document.*) Did you write this?
ADOLF (*After checking the exhibit.*): Yes.
PROSECUTOR: Is this your handwriting?
ADOLF: No.
PROSECUTOR: What do you mean, no?
ADOLF: I wasn't in Berlin on the date marked on the document.
PROSECUTOR: But the document was written in Munich.
ADOLF: I wasn't there either. At the time I was on duty in Dachau.
PROSECUTOR: What kind of duty?
ADOLF: On second thoughts, I was in Linz.
PROSECUTOR: So how does your signature appear on this document?
ADOLF: It's a later addition, although I would like to point out that the numbers on the document are somewhat illegible. The figure 4 is somewhat unclear and very much resembles a 7.
PROSECUTOR: So in your opinion twice two is seven?
ADOLF: I didn't say that. I'm not a mathematician. My remark referred only to the form of the figure 4, which reminds me of the figure 7 in Document 6013.
PROSECUTOR: Well, will you make up your mind?
ADOLF: I was in Dachau.

COURT PRESIDENT: Accused, you are requested to answer the question, how much is twice two?

ADOLF: Four.

PROSECUTOR: So it's not seven?

ADOLF: I didn't say seven. I only remarked that the form of the figure 4 reminds me in certain documents of the figure 7.

PROSECUTOR: We are not dealing here with "documents." All we are concerned with here is Document No. 6013.

ADOLF: I can't be responsible for this document, because on the date it was signed I was in Linz.

PROSECUTOR: So it is Linz after all, is it?

ADOLF: As far as these matters can be reconstructed.

PROSECUTOR: And I'm telling you that working out twice two never did constitute a problem for you!

ADOLF: May I point out that I'm not a mathematician.

PROSECUTOR: Will you please raise two fingers.

ADOLF (*Complies.*): I swear by Almighty God....

PROSECUTOR: I didn't ask you to take an oath. I only asked you to raise two fingers.

ADOLF: May I make a statement at this point?

PROSECUTOR: Go ahead.

ADOLF: Lopke was transferred to the Protectorate in the fall of 1943, and so Schultz could not possibly have met him in the Salzkammergut late that year.

PROSECUTOR: I don't quite see the connection.

ADOLF: I took an oath, sir, to tell only the truth. Lopke was not involved in Schultz's affairs.

PROSECUTOR: All right, he wasn't. The question is, how many fingers did Lopke raise?

ADOLF: To the best of my knowledge, Lopke never raised any fingers.

PROSECUTOR: I mean you! How many fingers are you raising now?

ADOLF: Two, I think. Though I cannot be held responsible for possible inaccuracies in this field. I never dealt with mathematics.

PROSECUTOR: Never mind. Now please raise two fingers of your other hand as well.

ADOLF (*Cooperates.*)

PROSECUTOR: Now count. How many fingers can you see?

ADOLF: Ten.

PROSECUTOR: I mean raised fingers.

ADOLF: But I can see those I didn't raise just as well.

PROSECUTOR: We are concerned only with your raised fingers.

ADOLF: Those which I didn't raise also belong to me. As a matter of fact, they represent sixty per cent of my total number of fingers; i.e. a fifty per cent majority compared to those raised, if I'm not mistaken.

PROSECUTOR: I want to know only one thing – what is the total number of your twice-two raised fingers?

ADOLF: Now?

PROSECUTOR: Yes. Count them.

ADOLF (*Tries but fails.*): I can't.

PROSECUTOR: Why not?

ADOLF: Because I'm accustomed to count by running a finger over the objects I'm counting. In this case here, I am confused by the fact that the finger I'm counting with is identical with the finger to be counted and this causes duplication. My oath obliges me to be extremely accurate. I request permission to make a statement.

COURT PRESIDENT: Go ahead.

ADOLF: I do not intend to create the impression that I am rejecting out of hand the version according to which twice two under certain circumstances can give results which approximate to four, but I would like to stress that I have never participated in this kind of research work, as this would have been considered an overstepping of well-defined competences. I request that Schultz's testimony be accepted here, because at that time he was Gauleiter in Wuppertal.

PROSECUTOR: I understand from your statement that you practically agree with Schultz insofar as twice two is concerned.

ADOLF: I have already said that I cannot be as explicit as all that as long as I'm testifying under oath. But I'm ready to bear all the consequences rather than create the impression that I intend to shirk my duty.

PROSECUTOR: All right, so twice two is four?

ADOLF: I already made a statement on this, if I'm not mistaken.

PROSECUTOR: I want to hear it again!

ADOLF: I already made a statement on this, if I'm not mistaken.

PROSECUTOR: I want to hear your statement again.

ADOLF: As you like. To the best of my knowledge, the result of the above mathematical computation is approximately what you, sir, said a few minutes ago.

PROSECUTOR (*Presses him against the wall.*): So its four!

ADOLF: As far as I can judge.

PROSECUTOR (*Presses.*): Four!

ADOLF: On general lines, apparently.

PROSECUTOR (*Presses.*): Twice two is four. Yes or no?

ADOLF: The former.

PROSECUTOR: Thank you. That's all I wanted to know.

☐ *And now a popular variation on the income tax theme, dedicated to our dear mentor, the famous economics professor C. Northcote Parkinson.*

Maximalists' Revolt

———☐———

Like all serious things, it started with a toothache. The dentist found that there was a hole in one of my molars, but in the middle of the treatment he turned off the drill and slipped out of his white smock.

"Sorry," he said. "It's not worth my while continuing."

I lay supine in his chair, my mouth pried wide open by a little springy instrument, groaning dejectedly.

"My net income reached Sh.1,000 a month this year," he said, and started stacking his instruments in their cabinet. "I am paying maximum tax at the rate of over eighty percent on every additional pound. It is not worth the trouble."

I motioned with my hands that I was for continuing the treatment regardless.

"It's not worth your while either, sir," the dentist coaxed me. "You have to earn Sh.3,000 to keep Sh.600 net with which to pay me. And after paying tax on that sum I'll be left with only Sh.120. I intended to pay this Sh.120 to my wife's driving teacher. In other words, out of your Sh.3,000 the teacher will actually get a total of Sh.24."

"All right," I said, "but that's net!"

"True," the dentist agreed, "but unfortunately our driving teacher doubled his fee as of yesterday and now asks Sh.48 net per lesson. So, to pay him the extra Sh.24 I now have to raise the fee you are paying for this treatment from Sh.3,000 to Sh.6,000. Come on, let's forget it."

I spat out the little springy instrument, got up and whispered the national slogan into the dentist's ear: "Listen, did I ask you for a receipt?"

"No, you are on the ball," the dentist agreed, "but I don't want any trouble. I declare all my income. It's a question of honor with me."

"So the hole in the tooth will have to stay?"

"No, you can pay Sh.48 net direct to my wife's driving teacher. If you do that we'll both be covered."

"Just a second," I thought out loud. "What am I going to say if the authorities discover in the driving teacher's books that I paid for your wife's lessons?"

"Tell them she's your lover?"

"May I see her photo?"

"I meant for taxation purposes only."

I asked him whether we could go on with the drilling, and we made a date for the end of the week. But then I ran into complications with the driving teacher. Seems he too is up to his ears in the maximum rate of tax.

"Sorry," the man informed me. "Until the end of August, I won't touch money, because each additional penny puts me in a higher tax bracket. Money is out of the question."

"So couldn't I pay your grocery bill?"

"It's already been paid by the furniture manufacturer, who is learning to drive his private car. I am quite well organized," the teacher added. "The house painter who studies the motorcycle with me, for instance, the other day painted my sister's apartment in lieu of a fee. My garage bill is jointly paid by two fashion designers. Can you sing?"

"Not really."

"That's a pity. I'd like to develop my voice. Do you have a stamp collection?"

"Only key rings."

"That's junk. But you know what? Pay our baby sitter in exchange for the driving lessons of your dentist's wife."

I got along nicely with the baby sitter. Although at first she was afraid of negotiating with me, saying she didn't accept money from strangers, I proposed bringing recommendations from our plumber, locksmith, seamstress, barber, gardener, electrician, beautician, general practitioner, lawyer and night watchman, all of whom can testify that I pay everything only in cash, without receipts, very discreetly and urbanely.

"No, I don't want to be in anybody's power," the baby sister persisted. "Is your tooth hurting badly?"

"It's getting worse all the time."

"Then buy me some contact lenses."

"Willingly," I agreed. "But what am I going to say if they discover it in the optician's books?"

"Tell them I am your mistress."

"Sorry, but that job is taken," I informed the baby sitter. "The dentist's wife has already registered with me. Do you have a raincoat?"

"Yes, the young couple upstairs with the newborn baby bought me one," said the babysitter. "I am willing to settle for a weekend in Tiberias with half board."

That sounded reasonable. Later on I learned that the contact lenses too would have worked, because lately several Tel Aviv opticians have started selling office supplies as well. In these shops the little taxpayer buys himself spectacles and gets an official receipt for office supplies which are tax-deductible. There are also new shops selling *objets d'art* and china statuettes linked to typewriters, and somewhere in the north of Tel Aviv there is a massage parlor where they give you receipts for typing and photocopying. Our Mediterranean people are quick to adapt themselves to the facts of life. Nor did I run into any particular maximum difficulties at the Tiberias hotel.

"I have a room over the weekend for the driving teacher's baby sitter," the boss said, "but not by telephone."

I drove down to Tiberias and discussed the matter privately, in an open field.

"All right, let's see." The boss leafed through a secret little notebook. "The first floor is taken by my son's music teacher. Next to him lives the owner of the laundry and in the royal suite my income tax adviser. Here everything is paid for in services and merchandise. It's not worthwhile taking money, because eighty percent...."

"I know, I know," I agreed. "But how am I going to pay you? Could I do some dishwashing?"

"There is no vacancy," said the hotel owner. "On the other hand I have an idea: pay my dentist."

And thus the circle closed. The hotel owner's dentist refused to accept money, because he too is in the maximum bracket, and asked for an air ticket to Uruguay for his mother-in-law, or 3,000 eggs and 10 kilos of salt. By then I was a little tired of the maximum pursuit and decided to resign myself to the toothache until I could locate through newspaper ads a bad dentist in a low tax bracket.

Anyway, the government's wise fiscal policy deserves unreserved praise for not only preventing bank liquidity but also for succeeding – for the first time in modern history – in eradicating that ancient curse of mankind and removing the evil of money as a means of payment. We have returned to the barter system of primitive peoples, a most praiseworthy development. Before long we shall return to the trees of the governmental jungle.

☐ *The latest government survey shows that, barring locusts, no single factor causes as much damage to our national economy as the uncontrolled sending of New Year greeting cards. The Ministry of Labor figures that some 30 million working days are wasted each year, both on addressing envelopes and on sorting them at the post office, not to mention the mailmen who drop like flies as the holidays approach.*

Stamping Out

——☐——

On these sultry mornings, the overburdened mailman is a common sight as he trudges through the dust of the metropolis carrying bags of half a ton and more....

"Folks," the Postmaster General pleads with us, "don't overdo this greeting card business!"

According to Bureau of Statistics figures, 60 percent of all addressees discard the Happy and Fruitful New Year without bothering to open the envelope; about 30 percent have a quick glance and then toss it away; the rest aren't sure. When one of the subjects, a rubber wholesaler who dispatched 4,009 Happy New Years, was asked to whom he had sent so many greetings, he answered: "Me, I sent? I don't remember...."

That is, the thing is done out of habit, as a kind of reflex movement of the hand muscles. Experts at the Central Post Office have calculated that if this year's Happies and Fruitfuls were placed end to end the column would reach Jaffa, circle that city twice, and return to Tel Aviv in an ambulance....

Then the authorities decided to stem this floodtide.

"All Israelis are brothers. There is no need to reaffirm this every year in writing," the Minister of Posts declared in a dramatic TV speech. "The Government is firmly resolved to put an end to this card game...."

A Government ordinance limiting the H & Fs to five per head was published in the Official Gazette, with two weeks' jail and a Sh.1,000 fine for violators. Sad to say, the public did not cooperate. On the eve of the holidays, 40 mailmen collapsed in the Northern District alone; of these, six had to be operated on for hernias, and one went out of his mind and keeps mumbling "fruitful, fruitful, fruitful" to this very day. An emergency survey revealed that the Israeli public is circumventing the order by putting their greeting cards inside sealed envelopes and sending them as ordinary mail, because it prefers to pay the higher tariff rather than renounce the Happies. What is more, many take advantage of the closed envelope to add a Creative and Productive and Great and Consolidating and Peaceful and Permanent Work Year.

"Murder," the Secretary of the Mailmen and Porters' Union declared. "We protest against this footslogging!"

A number of citizens appealed to the U.N. Secretary General about the violation of their greeting freedom. The authorities had no choice but to pass a new law forbidding the sending, with or without envelopes, of any and all New Year greetings, happy or otherwise. Penalties were raised to two years' jail. At the same time a task force was detailed to open every suspicious letter. Following these strong-arm policies several Tel Aviv citizens were arrested, among them an insurance broker who all by himself had sent out 2,600 Happy and Prosperous New Years within Safe and Recognized Borders.

The broker's attorney pleaded in court that in fact his client had only distributed "a political pamphlet," whereupon the Knesset amended the Greetings Interdiction Law, specially banning mention of the words "fruitful", "year" and "happy", during the two-month period preceding New Year's Day. As a result there was a sharp increase in attempts to hoodwink the authorities. A young Haifa architect, for instance, sent out 520 bar mitzvah form telegrams signed "Mrs. Happy Neujahr."

The penalty for illegal greetings was upped to 15 years with conditional hard labor, but that didn't help much either. A week before

New Year's Day the task force spotted a circular of the "Hapfroo" Agricultural Machinery Company Ltd. which aroused their suspicion by a sentence at the bottom: "Don't keep circular in refrigerated place." When the circular was placed over a flame, fat block letters appeared under the printed agricultural text: "May the Workers' Strength grow and may the Cooperative Idea triumph Next Year! This is the wish of Miriam and Elhanan Gross, Herzliya."

The couple, a co-op manager and his wife, got eight years. The Government sealed all mailboxes in the country for a month and called out a people's militia to guard them. Every citizen who came to a post office had to present his ID card and make a sworn declaration that his postal effects did not contain greetings of any kind or description. Transgressors were court-martialed. A confrontation between the authorities and the population seemed inevitable. . . .

"The sending of H & Fs has risen by nine percent," the Minister of Posts announced before handing in his resignation, "a third of the Gross National Product. . . ." Civil war was in the air. In a number of Haifa suburbs, rowdies forced the mailman to distribute about 1,000 New Year calendars. On the outskirts of Tel Aviv an occasional rat-tat-tat can be heard of an evening and everybody knows that another attempt is being made to send out greeting cards. Armored cars are prowling the provinces and there's a rumor we're going to have three successive leap years with the holidays removed. That's how matters stand at the moment in this poor country gripped by the holiday fever. Happy . . . oops!

☐ *We must never forget that we are the People of the Book and have been since the world began — an event, by the way, that was first described with reliable detail only in the Hebrew edition. Accordingly we make our children learn the Old Testament by heart — verse by verse, letter by letter, comma by comma. What's more, we hold an annual Bible Quiz in Jerusalem each Independence Day to see who knows the Book of Jeremiah with the greatest verbatim accuracy. The Prophet himself never made it to the finals.*

THE QUIZ

———☐———

The Posts have played a distinguished part in our history, due to the fact that the Jewish People dwelt in the Diaspora and communication between the dispersed tribes was essential to its existence as a national entity. No wonder, then, that a wave of emotion swept the Israeli public when the Ministry of Posts announced a National Telephone Quiz, to be held in conjunction with the Ministry of Education and Culture.

The preliminaries were held on a country-wide scale, and the top candidates gathered for the finals at the National Convention Hall. A radio announcer broadcast a running account of the excited crowd flocking toward the hall, while the rest of the population huddled around their sets at home, armed with a telephone directory. The four finalists sat on the stage basking in the unreserved admiration of the entire audience. Everyone knew what profundity of learning, what acute brain, incisive logic and sense of orientation had brought these four so far. Their names were household words by now: Glick the computer engineer, Tovah, a switchboard operator and the public's darling, Professor Doctor Birnboim from the Faculty of Electronic Brains, and the poet Tola'at-Shani, descendant of a long line of chess players. I confess that I, too, was among the crowd at the entrance trying to catch a glimpse of the stars. The atmosphere was festive although tense, and even members of the diplomatic corps were unable to hide their mounting excitement. The Minister of Posts opened the proceedings with an erudite speech: "This is the first time in 2,000 years that free and unfettered Jews have held a contest of this nature in their own National Convention Hall," said the Minister, and went on to draw an inspired historical background, describing postal functions from Noah's dove through Abraham's angels and the Babylonian Epistles, up to the intriguing question about Persian Jewry and what would have happened to it had Haman been able, God forbid, to send his commands by phone instead of lazy couriers.... Afterward the youth champion was introduced to the audience, who received the bespectacled lad with melting glances.

"A real whizz kid," the fellow next to me said. "I hear he knows the number of every pharmacy!"

"In the world?"

"Nah!"

My neighbor's tone conveyed the abysmal ignorance my question revealed. The contest, he explained, was of a purely local nature. That is, we would concentrate on the Israeli phonebook from the topographical-factual aspect. It's true that last year's quiz had been held in an international framework, and the presence of foreign contestants had obliged the judges to stick to questions of a secondary nature, like who invented the telephone, how does a switchboard work, or where does the transatlantic cable go. Tonight's contest, however, was strictly regional, enabling us to devote our attention to essentials, that is to say to phone numbers....

The chairman of the judges' panel, our university rector, posed the scintillating questions, which had been formulated by a special board of scholars in over half a year of strenuous brain work. The first question rang through the tense silence of the auditorium: "What is the first number on page 478, Haifa?"

Engineer Glick's reply came promptly, his lips curling in a faint smile: "Weinstock, Moshe. 12 Tel-Hai Street, 40572!"

Breathlessly the audience turned the pages of their phonebooks, and when the answer proved correct a storm of applause broke out in the hall. Soon enough, however, it turned out that questions like that were just by way of warming up before the real fight, and our four walking phonebooks tackled them with the greatest of ease. Only Tovah produced a sensation when in answer to the rector's question, "How many Goldenblooms are there in Tel Aviv?" she said, "Six."

"Sorry," said the rector, "I see only five."

"Uhu," said Tovah, "but there's a sixth in the Appendix: Goldenbloom, Ephraim. 22 Levi-Izhak Street, 27916."

The rector turned to the last pages and exclaimed, visibly moved: "You're right!"

My ears went pink with admiration. Never, never had I watched people whose learning encompassed such horizons. Still, Professor Doctor Birnboim was defeated by the next question, and even the poet Tola'at-Shani hit upon the right answer only at the very last moment. The question was: "Which number on Gordon Street, Tel Aviv, has three zeros?"

"Got it!" shouted the poet, the veins on his forehead bulging, "Wexler, Viola. Voice Training: 2-0-7-0-0!"

Tola'at-Shani's memory failed him when it came to the number of Viola's house on Gordon Street, but according to the rules of the game, complex questions didn't require a full address. Tola'at-Shani got two points and a round of applause. Tovah demonstrated her prowess again when it came to quoting chapter and verse: "The text on Page 53, Jerusalem?" she repeated with characteristic nonchalance. "Dial Correctly and Avoid Errors!"

Engineer Glick, on the other hand, flunked a childishly easy one that any amateur phonebook fan would have known: "What advertisement appears on Page 356, Tel Aviv?" (T. Pfefferman, Butcher.)

Indeed, at this stage of the great match all four contestants were beginning to show the first signs of mental wear and tear. Professor Doctor Birnboim's time ran out again while he racked his brains for the answer to: "Which phone number has a middle figure that equals the difference between its two first and two last figures?"

The Professor dropped out of the running at this point and Glick took the question. Sprawled back in his chair with exhaustion he whispered: "Gardosh, Shoshanna. Tel Aviv, Page 180, first column, 29th number from top: 2-3-1-3-4-!"

The overwhelmed audience responded with a thunderous ovation, and I too clapped my hands, even though bizarre thoughts were nagging at my brain: "Please," I turned to my neighbor, "actually, what's the good of knowing every number in the phonebook?"

"What do you mean?" said my neighbor indignantly. "What do you mean what's the good?"

"Don't get me wrong, sir. The directory is a vital work of reference and I'm sure we couldn't live without it for a single day. I'd be the last to deny its fundamental importance to us all. I'm just asking why learn it by heart when you can always find what you're looking for right there?"

"You talk like a child," my neighbor grinned. "What would you do if you found yourself in the desert without a phonebook?"

"I wouldn't have a phone either."

"Let's say you would."

"I'd ask Information."

"Ssh," said my neighbor, "let me listen."

But at this point the whole neighborhood intervened in heated whispers. All around me honest Jews were trying to show me the error of my ways. The team, they explained, are mental giants. While other people waste their time and dissipate their intellectual powers on all kinds of scientific hair-splitting and dubious research, the phone masters dedicate themselves from the age of three to one single purpose: the study of each letter, each figure, each printing error, each stain and wrinkle in the Hebrew directory, till they attain a perfection that must earn them the respect and veneration of all men.

On stage, meanwhile, the final rounds were being played.

Engineer Glick performed miracles in solving the problem: "If you should stick a pin into the third figure on line 4, column 3, Page

421, which figures will it run through on the following pages?" Glick got as far as Petach Tikvah, Page 605, when the pin gave out.

The audience held its breath all through, and only when the last correct figure came did it let go in a storm of cheers and whistles. My neighbor muttered, "Glory be to God!" and most people wept unashamedly. The rector asked for silence and said that before announcing the winners he wanted to offer the question sent in by the Prime Minister. A hush fell over the audience.

"Well then," asked the rector, "how does one make a phone call?"

The team sank into a bewildered silence. Tovah mumbled something about holes and plugs, but it soon became apparent that this unexpected problem had the champs stumped. After a hurried consultation the poet Tola'at-Shani announced in the name of the whole team that they considered this provocative question went beyond the framework of the contest, as it couldn't be answered in figures. The rector saved the hour by declaring Glick "1984 Phonebook Champion." Tovah was runner-up. The cheering crowd surged toward the stage and carried their idols out on their shoulders. I remained behind, thinking I ought to phone home and give them the results, but for the life of me I couldn't remember my number.

☐ *In our country a Philharmonic Orchestra subscription is a first-rate status symbol. One may say that it is a matter of honor for anyone who can afford to buy his wife an evening dress from one of the exclusive couturiers, or else is himself an exclusive couturier or an industrialist. Or has a successful export-import business. And a slight cold.*

THE PHILHARMONIC COUGH

―――☐―――

Getting our subscription was child's play, really. Originally it had been bought by Mr. S., director of the orchestra fund, who subsequently embezzled 20,000 shekels and drew two years. With the breadwinner behind bars, hard times descended on Mrs. S., and she found herself forced to auction off the orphaned subscription so as to pay her husband's debts, which ran into many thousands. The ticket passed to the exporter T.L., who bid sky-high because he did not hear the auctioneer, being stone-deaf. At the end of the very first season T.L. divorced his wife. Under the terms of the settlement the children stayed with the father, the subscription with the mother.

From here on, events took a criminal turn; that is, the former Mrs. L. suddenly died, poisoned, and two months later her subtenant, a certain engineer G., was caught at the Mann Auditorium, suspiciously sitting in the deceased's seat. The ill-fated subscription was impounded by the Supreme Court and raffled off among the members of the Cabinet. (The Minister of Posts won.) So we did not get *that* subscription. But our neighbors, the Seligs, went abroad and left us theirs.

The beginning of the season's third concert was more or less routine. The players tuned their instruments (why can't they do it at home?), and the conductor was given a warm ovation. He needed it badly, as the sudden winter storm howling outside had frozen all of us to the marrow. The conductor took the obbligato bow as he stepped on stage, and the marvelous strains of Tchaikovsky's Pathétique filled the hall. The execution was not at all bad, but the concert did not really get under way until the end of the first movement. That is, during the reprise of the strings, from the front rows and the throat of a middle-aged knitted-goods manufacturer there suddenly came a sonorous cough. It was a sort of barking, sforzando cough, tempered by a certain amount of emotional tremolo, proof, if proof were needed, that the performer not only had a complete command of the throat-rasping technique but also possessed a tempestuous musical bent.

Obviously, this was the evening's real curtain-raiser.

The catarrhic middle rows and the sniffling sextets in the balcony, inspired by the clashing cadenza, joyously fell in with a throaty presto passage which filled the hall with animated ensemble coughing of natural but nasal beauty, warmth and glow.

Outstanding in this passage was the owner of a well-known perfumery sitting near the aisle, who demonstrated an amazing virtuosity on her trumpet-like organ and produced mellifluous sordino effects through the adroit use of her handkerchief. The intonation of this accomplished soloist was somewhat brassy in spots, but breathtakingly precise, clear, factual and yet ... exciting. Her husband and accompanist, seated next to her, provided the contrapuntal motif with a limpid throat-clearing which sometimes bordered on the pathetic but was totally devoid of bathos.

These were moments of highest spiritual uplift. My neighbors, a somewhat reticent couple of fanatic music lovers, coughed with exemplary consequentialness, interpreting the score lying open on their knees.

"Pam-pam" – a tempo moderato cough. "Pim-pim" – a molto vivace sneeze.

I sat there with the little one, listening raptly, although the orchestra on stage provided a jarring contrast to the harmonious tutti sneezing.

Undeniably, that *je ne sais quoi* which makes all the difference between an ordinary concert and an unforgettable evening was very much present in the hall.

The next item on the program, a pallid Sibelius symphony, was somewhat drowned out by the polyphonic rattling of the ecstatic audience, but the total effect of organic oneness was complete. As for myself, I waited for a quarter's rest in the wheezing poem as the players filled their lungs in preparation for an extra flourish, and at the right moment rose somewhat in my seat, cleared my throat and let go with a recitative and highly expressive cough which revealed the sum total of my musical personality.

The effect was electrifying. Not only did the conductor beam at me, visibly pleased, and stop the orchestra lest it interfere with the concert out front, but he even cued the entrance of the soloist in the first row, a successful real estate broker, who repeated the main theme in a hammering coda. Under the maestro's baton, the man produced remarkable bravura in sneezing. Bending double in his seat, he executed a series of expressive arpeggios on his crackling vocal cords, with the main theme taking on a more virile, martial timbre while the accompanying wheezes left his lungs in trills, by turns lyrically soft and raucously powerful, sometimes even shrill. It had been a long time since the Mann Auditorium resounded to such suggestive coughing, reminding one of a growling volcano erupting in a delicate Levantine miniature. The ensemble in the hall, despite its youthful vigor, felt itself carried away and yielded to this inimitable performer for whom the difficult art of concert coughing obviously held no secrets.

The well-selected program ended with a crescendo on the gamut of unison coughing, a piece of unexcelled authenticity leaving no room for phoney romanticism but offering practically boundless scope for individual snorts and the display of the utmost instrumental virtuosity on handkerchiefs, scarves, neckties and inhalation apparati.

An impressive evening of spectacular works and flawless performance.

Counsel for the Defense

One night last week, in the early-morning hours, a cop materialized on the doorstep of my residence and handed me a summons to go to the police station next day at 8 A.M. The little woman took one look at it and blanched. Not as though there were any cause for alarm – of course not, but still. . . .

"Why are they summonsing you in such a hurry?" the wife asked, puzzled. "Are you in trouble with the law?"

"I?" I said. "Don't be ridiculous!"

The woman threw me an oblique glance.

"In any case," she urged me, "don't go there alone. Take a lawyer."

"What for?"

"I don't know what for. I just want someone to be with you there lest you get in trouble."

For the first time in her life the woman had used the word "lest" and that completely demoralized me.

Later in the day I called on Shay-Sheinkrager, the noted jurist who is acknowledged as one of the best brains in the state. Shay-Sheinkrager listened to the details of my case, meditated for a while, then announced that he was willing to undertake my defense. I felt greatly relieved. I signed the necessary papers, which went into force immediately.

Next morning I took somewhat apprehensive leave of my wife and, accompanied by my lawyer, went to the police station. We were received by the desk officer, a heavily mustachioed young man. When Shay-Sheinkrager gave him my summons, the cop stuck his hand in the desk drawer and pulled out my briefcase, which I had lost a few months earlier.

"We found your briefcase, sir," the cop said, smiling engagingly. "You can have it back now."

"Thank you very much," I said to the policeman. "Very kind of you."

And with that I grabbed the truant briefcase and prepared to leave in high spirits. Not so my lawyer.

"Very touching," he remarked. "May I ask you, Mr. Desk Officer, what makes you so sure that this is my client's property?"

"What a question," the duty officer grinned. "We found a laundry bill in it with the gentleman's name and address."

"My dear man," said my lawyer, "didn't it occur to you that the case could be the property of the laundry?"

"But it *is* mine," I assured my lawyer. "I recognized it right away from the yogurt stain on its side."

"Kindly keep out of this," Shay-Sheinkrager remarked politely but firmly. "Mr. Desk Officer, I request that you write out a report!"

"What report? Take the briefcase and be gone!"

"Really," I joined in, "what else have we got to do here?"

My attorney stepped back and stared out the window for several moments, then he turned on his heel and snapped at us, "I'll tell you, gentlemen, what else we have to do here! Don't you think we ought to see what's inside the briefcase?"

Silence. How silly of me not to have thought of that. That's where a lawyer's perspicacity comes in.

"Ough!" the cop sighed and prepared to open the briefcase. "So what's the problem?"

"*No!*" my lawyer's voice whipcracked. "I object! I request that the exhibit be opened in the presence of an official witness!"

The cop twirled his mustache nervously and went to call his sergeant. Both were red-faced when they returned.

"Sir," the lawyer said to me, "now kindly make up a detailed list of the objects which – to the best of your knowledge – are in the attached briefcase."

"Willingly," I said. "But I don't remember."

"So there is nothing we can do," the sergeant said and prepared to open the exhibit, but my attorney pounced on him.

"Though it is true that my client claims he does not remember what is in the briefcase," he said, "that does not mean that he admits the complete absence of valuables at the time of the loss!"

The cops looked at us, their brows furrowed. S.-S. pulled me aside.

"Please don't say a word without consulting me! Let me handle this!"

He then drafted the report in dry but lucid legalese: "According to the statement of my client, and without prejudicing his rights as the sole and legal owner of the found object, he is unable, owing to a lapse of memory, to testify to the effect that this briefcase, which on the date of the signature is located at the present police station, whose representative admits that to the best of his knowledge the attached briefcase constitutes the property of my client, and which object was found a number of days ago...."

"Just a moment," the sergeant interrupted him and called his officer from the adjacent room. That worthy came out in a visibly bad mood, but before he could say a word, Shay-Sheinkrager introduced himself and demanded fair treatment in this miserable affair. The atmosphere was tense with excitement.

"Sir," my attorney addressed me, "it is my duty to inform you that from here on, anything you say may be used against you at the trial."

I asked him whether I'd have to take an oath, but S.-S. assured me that we had not yet reached that stage. We initialed the report and S.-S. solemnly announced: "My client no longer objects to the opening of the briefcase."

The officer put his hand in the briefcase and pulled out a pencil.

"Sir," the attorney called out, stressing each syllable, "is this your pencil?"

I looked at it. It was small and the worse for wear. A very ordinary pencil.

"How do I know?" I said. "I can't remember."

S.-S.'s eyes lit up with a holy fire.

"Gentlemen," he announced. "Let's keep a cool head. Are you quite sure, sir, that you cannot remember the exhibit as coming from among your writing implements?"

"I told you I don't."

"Then I demand that the Police District Commander be notified forthwith."

"The District Commander?" the officer fumed. "For heaven's sake, what for?"

"Sir! If the 'honest finder' placed a pencil in the briefcase, he could just as well have removed objects from it."

The District Commander arrived blinking his eyes impatiently.

"What's the matter?" he asked. "Oh, no, it's not you again, Shay-Sheinkrager!"

My lawyer walked up and down the room for a while, then pulled up in front of the District Commander and said, in an emotion-laden voice, "In the name of my client, I am suing the finder of the lost briefcase, and accuse him on the following counts: (a) Unlawful use of our chattels; (b) Removal of our property from it."

"Just a moment," the District Commander snorted. "Are you insinuating a theft here?"

"If you must know, I am! My client claims with reasonable certainty, and beyond the shadow of a doubt, that an undetermined theft has taken place."

"All right," the District Commander sighed. "Who found this briefcase?"

The sergeant rummaged through his papers.

"The policeman on the beat found it."

The District Commander turned on me. "Sir, are you accusing a policeman of theft?"

"Don't answer him!" S.-S. jumped up. "Don't say a word! They are out for your blood. I know their tricks! Sir," he then addressed the District Commander, "we have nothing to add to what we have said, and will testify only before a properly appointed court!"

"As you like!" the District Commander said. "I hope you realize that you are insulting a public servant?"

"Objection!" S.-S. roared. "This is blackmail!"

"Oh!" the District Commander roared back. "Insulting a uniformed policeman on official duty? Section 8 of the Criminal Code!"

"Objection! I refer to Appendix 47 of the Law for the Protection of the Policeman's Rights as published in Official Gazette No. 317!"

"Let the court decide," the District Commander said and turned to me. "In any case you, sir, are under arrest."

My lawyer saw me to the cell door.

"Don't worry," he reassured me. "They can't do a thing to you. They have no incriminating material against you. We are going to prove the policeman's guilt. We'll ask for an order *nisi* against the Police Minister. Let him come and explain why the honest finder was not arrested. Have a good night's rest – I'll phone your wife."

I shook his hand warmly. A lonely prisoner's best friend is his lawyer. Only then did I realize how fortunate I was to have such a brilliant lawyer. I'm sure he'll get me out on bail.

The Bedside Manner

―――□―――

It started with a strange, empty feeling in the pit of my stomach,[1] followed by a deep, inner rumbling. At first I did not pay any attention, but when the symptoms became fairly frequent, especially after I had not eaten anything for six or eight hours, I became alarmed and asked my maiden aunt for advice. She insisted that I see a doctor at once.

"All right," I said. "I'll go to the Sick Fund."[2]

"Are you crazy?" my aunt snorted. "All the Sick Fund knows is how to take your money. Besides, it's just one big factory. Go and see Professor Grosslockner."

"Who's that?"

"You are joking, of course. You want me to believe you never heard of Grosslockner the miracle worker, the savior of hundreds of thousands?"

"Hundreds of thousands? Come, come."

"Don't come-come me! When I say hundreds of thousands, I mean hundreds of thousands. Go and see him, speak German, and

---

[1] You have to be extra careful with your stomach in the tropics, especially when eating at Oriental restaurants, which faithfully cling to the Arab tradition that there is no sense in keeping the place clean as everything depends on Allah anyway.

[2] The Sick Fund is one of Israel's largest enterprises, in which half a million healthy shareholders make monthly investments. The only time this excellent institution is not quite up to scratch is when the shareholder falls sick. It then offers fairly adequate, but by no means lavish, hospital treatment.

It is related that at one of the hospitals there was a patient who had undergone stomach surgery, and whose tormenting pangs of hunger the doctors were trying to relieve by hypnosis.

"You are now eating nice potato soup," the doctor suggested. "A whole plateful of nourishing potato soup."

"Why don't you suggest something better?" a sympathetic nurse asked. "Let's say chicken casserole with French fries and lettuce salad."

"Sorry," said the doctor. "This is a Sick Fund patient."

don't worry. He'll find some serious disease."

"All right," I said, intending to start out for the miracle worker, but my aunt informed me that one had to make an appointment first. I phoned the professor and a female voice told me to come three weeks from Tuesday at 5:26 P.M. "Until then please don't eat, drink, sleep, or smoke."

I found the doctor's door open and fifty or sixty patients crowding the huge, baroque waiting room. My greeting went unanswered because all were in a state of almost religious awe.

It took me less than half an hour to realize how the doctor's monster practice was being run. Doors leading out of the waiting room opened and closed, white-clad nurses scurried hither and thither, from time to time half-naked men scampered through the room, then three patients would be lined up and marched into the medical sanctum. I was marveling at the staff's clocklike efficiency when a nurse came and asked me to follow her.

We stepped into the office, where the nurse opened a big ledger and took my particulars. Name? Born? (Yes.) Country of origin? Profession?

"Journalist," I said, to which the nurse replied: "Ninety-six shekels, please."

"Beg your pardon?"

"Ninety-six shekels."

"Why so much?"

"That's the fee for the first visit," said the nurse. "Only colleagues and members of related professions get a reduction."

"Fine," I said. "I am also a typewriter repair man."

The nurse said, "Just a moment," and entered the sanctum. When she came back, she said: "Ninety-five and a half shekels."

I plunked down the reduced fee and returned to my post in the waiting room. Hardly an hour and a half later, another nurse came and quickly led me into the adjoining bedroom. As she looked like a kind, homely person, I dared to ask her why the old boy was charging such exorbitant fees.

"My husband is not a philanthropic institution," Mrs. Grosslockner answered, then opened a big ledger and asked me in an icy voice what was the matter with me.

Now, this may sound strange, but I don't like to converse with women about my shortcomings. Especially not in bedrooms. I refused to tell her, and she sent me back to my roost, from where I could observe the ever-increasing traffic. Nurses were still dashing about, patients in tow.

"I say, sir," I said to my neighbor, "where does he get all these nurses from?"

"They are all Grosslockners," my neighbor answered. "The professor has seven sisters and two brothers. All are working here at the plant."

One of the brothers came and led me into the bathroom. He gave me a test tube and asked me to do something which prompted me to ask, "Why?" He replied that one can never know; these tests will have to be made before the professor admits me into his presence. No sooner had I finished than a sister came and dragged me into the kitchen. Blood and stomach juice. Back to base where I sat until nightfall, when another sister came and ordered me and two other patients to strip to our waists, not leave our seats, and be ready to move at a moment's notice. It was rather cold in the room and our teeth started chattering. The nurse told us she was sorry if she was causing us any hardship, but the professor's valuable time could not be wasted.

"I'm going to brief you," she said. "To save time, please refrain from greeting, immediately be seated on the three chairs standing in the middle of the room, breathe deeply, and stick out your tongues. Remain in that position until further notice. No need to bother the professor with questions and remarks; he knows everything from your files. Should he honor one of you with a question, please don't answer, or if this cannot be avoided, answer in one principal clause with a maximum of two words. Out again without greeting. Now repeat what I told you."

We recited the rules. The door of the sanctum opened and a

nurse whistled softly.

"Now!" our nurse shouted. "At the double!"

We doubled in (why don't they install a conveyor belt?) and did as we had been told. The professor passed us in review and leafed through our tongues. At that moment the door opened, the oldest sister came in and asked: "Diver?"

"Ninety-three pounds," the professor said, then asked me what diseases there had been in my family.

"Diverse," I answered (one word).

"How old are you?"

"Fifty." (In fact my age is fifty-five, but I didn't want to waste his time.)

With his miracle-working hand, the professor then prodded my back and asked what I felt.

"Back-prodding," I replied, and then Professor Grosslockner arrived at his diagnosis.

"Mr. Kleiner!" he said. "Your spine really needs treatment!"

"Excuse me," my neighbor remarked, though he could hardly speak with his tongue sticking out. "I am Kleiner."

"Don't interrupt me!" The professor jumped on him, angered by the man's jabbering. He then came back and informed me that I had a slight cold, probably contracted from sitting scantily clad in unheated rooms.

The professor prescribed two aspirins, then motioned us to get out. The other two wanted to say something, but the nurses pushed them out bodily.

One of the patients, a narrow-chested little man, complained while we dressed that he was in fact only the mailman and had tried to deliver a registered letter. He said this was the third time they had pushed him into the waiting room in spite of his protests. Last Monday he had even been on his way to the hospital for an appendectomy and had escaped from the ambulance just in the nick of time.

WHISTLE STOP

———□———

On Wednesday I went to the new neighborhood swimming pool. I had heard it was simply out of this world: small but spotless because they kept it spotless, and noiseless because there was no noise. There was quiet and order and national discipline and hygiene and politeness and rapport and obeying-of-administrative-orders and water and air and sun and shade and trees.

So curiosity got the better of me and I went to the new pool to check up on the rumors. I descended a number of well-scrubbed steps and had to admit that the legend was based on fact. The water was as transparent as a hidden tax, there wasn't a scrap of paper on the ground, no shouting, no horseplay, no hanky-panky of any kind. Culture reigned supreme, positively Scandinavian civilization. I tiptoed up to the ticket booth and said to its beauteous keeper: "A ticket please."

"Shalom, sir," the beauteous said. "We say Shalom here."

I said "Shalom", blushing deeply, and paid for the esthetically-designed, attractively-colored ticket. Then I turned to go to the locker room, but was stopped dead in my tracks by an ear-shattering whistle: "Frrr-frrr," and saw the lifeguard blowing in my general direction with a double-barreled, long-range whistle.

"Kindly change into bathing trunks in the locker room."

"Naturally," I answered, "that's what I came for."

"Then hurry, sir, will you," the lifeguard said, and turned his back on me to survey the pool area with eagle eyes, like a searchlight they'd forgotten to turn off in the morning. I quickly undressed in the locker room, hung my things on a brand-new plastic hanger, and handed them over to the young attendant, who addressed me in a most courteous way, saying: "Please button up your shirt, sir, otherwise it might fall off the hanger, and that would be a pity, wouldn't it?"

Full of gratitude I buttoned up the shirt, then accepted a perfectly round disk from the hands of the noble youth, who took this opportunity to wish me a pleasant time and good health. I left the locker room in a slight daze, but had hardly gone a few steps when I heard "Frrr-frrr!" and the lifeguard informed me that it was forbidden to enter the pool area in sandals, because of various summer fungi. Without arguing I slipped them off and carried them in my hands, but the lifeguard's whistle quickly reached me: "Frrr-frrr! Sandals may not be carried into the pool area."

I had no choice but to deposit my footwear with the noble youth, then emerged again. There was another "Frrr-frrr" and the lifeguard dropped a subtle hint: "Wouldn't you like to take a shower?"

In other words, it is forbidden to enter the pool area without showering. I was still standing under the shower when I heard a whistle which went something like this: "Frrr-frrr!"

Not only that, but the lifeguard left his high perch and came down to me in person.

"Sir," the descending lifeguard observed, "excuse me, but the elastic in your trunks is loose. Kindly get yourself another pair that won't slip."

I asked him how he knew that my elastic had stretched, whereupon he explained that he'd been in the profession for 15 years and had developed a sixth sense for loose rubber bands in the pool area. Then he returned to his perch, and I went to the beauteous, said "Shalom," and enquired about a pair of trunks, largish but slip-proof. I came out of the office and heard somebody whistling: "Frr-frr."

Before long I realized that the lifeguard had whistled to me to take another shower, because if you leave the pool area even for a moment, you revert to newcomer status. I showered and then dropped into one of the deck chairs lined up there in military order, and sure enough, "Frr-frr!" no sitting around the pool in wet swimsuits. I slunk away and started eating a cheese sandwich to restore my strength, but never got as far as the cheese because after one bite I heard a familiar "Frr-frr!" and the lifeguard motioned that eating around the pool is forbidden. He summoned a slave boy who shooed me away and sprinkled disinfectant around my deck chair.

It was then that the first wave of persecution mania struck me. I crawled away and hid behind a big concrete boulder in such a way that I could only see the sky, and no one on earth could see me. Lulled into a sense of security I fell asleep, but was immediately awakened by a shrill whistle.

"Frr-frr!" the lifeguard shrilled and shook me gently. "No sleeping in the pool area, you might get sunstroke. Into the water with you!"

I got up and hurried waterward, but on the way there was whistled at: "Frr-frr! First to the toilet!"

"I don't need to."

"Go!"

I went to the toilet, stayed there for two or three minutes, came out and made a swift dash for the water hoping for once to beat the man to it, but no.

"Frr-frr, don't run!"

It was the whistle-guard. What's more, he asked me to come close and inspected me all over for signs of leprosy. Satisfied that I was cured and no longer contagious, he sent me to the shower room. There, standing under the water with closed eyes, the suspicion flashed through my mind that I had stumbled into hell all unawares, but hadn't recognized it because it was camouflaged as a Scandinavian swimming pool. Musing on my predicament I walked without running toward the pool and prepared to dive in.

"Frr-frr!" the whistle promptly sounded. "No diving from the side in the pool area."

"Damn it!" I shouted. "What *is* allowed here?"

"Frr-frr!" the lifeguard replied. "No swearing in the pool area."

I fled from his side, dived in and swam underwater till my lungs nearly burst, hoping he'd forget about me, but he followed my movements like a hawk because, as I said, the water was transparent.

"Frr-frr!" he whistled as I came up for air. "No swimming with open eyes in the pool area. The water is chlorinated."

So I swam with closed eyes.

"Frr-frr! No splashing in the pool area."

"I can't help it, that's the way I swim."

"Frr-frr! Then stop swimming!"

I stopped swimming and drowned. As a matter of fact, that's what I should have done to begin with.

☐ *In our country it is difficult for a man to engage in sports. For skiing there is no snow to speak of; for ice skating the only ice available is found in the freezers of our refrigerators; gymnastics are boring, golf is anti-social and it is too hot for tennis. So all that is left is swimming. But the weather is too humid even for that.*

CAREFUL, SHALLOW WATER

———☐———

My son stands on the swimming pool steps and bawls. "Come into the water!"

"I'm scared!"

For the past half hour I've tried to coax my little redhead to let his daddy teach him to swim, but he is scared. Amir's fearsome crying is still in low gear but going strong. One could say it's very promising. I'm not angry with my baby. I remember only too well how my daddy, too, tried to teach me to swim, and I stood there on the steps of the swimming pool and cried my heart out. In the meantime educational methods have improved somewhat. Far be it from me to force my boy to do something against his will. He'll have to take the decisive step toward the conquest of the waves all by himself. Like a royal eaglet leaving the parental eyrie for the first time, he'll need only a light shove. Nature will do the rest, even if it be a rotten nature. Understanding, kindness and lots and lots of love, that's what a devoted father has to lavish in such a situation.

"Look, look," I say to my kitten, "the water hardly reaches up to your navel. I'm holding you tight. What can happen to you?"

"I'm scared."

"All the kids in the pool are laughing, playing, only you are crying. Why are you crying?"

"I'm scared."

"Are you stupid or weaker than the other kids?"

"Yes!"

Amir admitted this freely, unreservedly. A quick look around: the lifeguard is watching me from under his straw hat; scoffing parents are pointing us out to their frolicking brats. Before my mind's eye there appears a sinking ship, all the passengers waiting patiently in line for the captain's instructions, and then a burly, red-haired man elbows his way through the the crowd of women and children and plumps himself down in the first lifeboat. This is my son who didn't learn how to swim from his daddy.

"What are you scared of?"

"Of sinking."

"How can you sink in five inches of water? How?"

"I'm scared."

This child is allergic to water.

"Even if you wanted to you couldn't sink." I appeal to his intellect. "The body has a low specific gravity, so it floats on water. Look!"

Daddy lies down on the water and floats nicely on his back. It is most instructive, but just then some fool dives straight on my head and my mouth fills with water. I splutter, my specific gravity drowns, and my son bawls on the steps in third gear.

I enlist government help. "Mr. Lifeguard, tell him! Could anybody sink here in the children's pool?"

"And how," Straw Hat says. "You bet!"

Any other daddy would by now have dragged his son bodily into the pool, but not me, no sir. I love my son, despite his shortcomings, despite his inarticulate howls. What's more, I never loved him more than now, just because he shakes so much, because he looks so helpless, so stupid, damn it.

"Come, let's make a gentleman's agreement," I propose. "I won't touch you. You'll walk in up to your knees. If you like it, you stay. If you don't, you get out and that's that. O.K?"

My son bawls but takes a hesitant step forward. Result: doesn't like it, doesn't stay, gets the hell out and that's that. Amir is again on dry land. This time his bawling is legitimate. He also sounds muted shrieks and now and then yells "Mummy."

"Amir," I say to him, "if you don't get in right away, there won't be any TV tonight!"

Now that was too severe. My son bawls even in reverse. The pool water becomes distinctly salty.

"But look how simple it is." I demonstrate. "You stretch out your arms and count: one, two, three . . . four. . . ."

All right, I can't both swim and count. No one ever taught me. I am not a swimmer. I am only a writer. Amir stands on the stairs and escalates. A fun-loving crowd has gathered around us. I jump out of the pool and my son flees for his life, his bawling at maximum volume, but I catch him in an iron grip. I drag him back to teach him swimming of his own free will.

"Mummy," my son cries, "I'm scared!"

I have a strange feeling of *déjà vu*. Yes, yes, my father too had dragged me like this into the pool and I too had yelled desperately, "*Anyukám!*" Such is life; the clash of generations is inevitable. The fathers eat sour grapes and their sons bawl.

"Not water!" my son bawls. "Not water, Mummy!"

I'm holding him in the air about a yard above the water and he claims, crying, that he is drowning.

"One, two, three," I order, "swim!"

The child cries but goes through the motions. This is encouraging, but what's the use? I'm not trying to teach him to fly. I lower the eaglet cautiously to water level. He fights for his life, switches to colloquial Arabic, but I am stronger, because I am an athletic type.

"Swim!" I hear myself roaring. "One, two, three. . . ."

He bit me! He bit the hand which feeds him, or rather the hand which right now is quenching his thirst, with his mouse-teeth he bit the hand of his father who has shown him nothing but love ever since he was born! I catch him between my legs and fix his shaking hips in a steel vise. I force his hands forward and then back, one, two, three. I'll make him swim, even if he drinks up the whole pool in the process.

"Don't . . . be . . . afraid!"

One day he'll thank me that I taught him to rule the waves. But right now he kicks. His feet, relatively free, beat a tattoo on my back, in time with his bawls. My son's face is distorted with crying. He has aged a whole day in just one hour. I push him deep into the water. So he's drinking a little water. Let him drink the Pacific Ocean for all I care. My father too had been held like this between his father's muscular legs. *Swim!* I can't remember when I last felt such anger toward any creature. What is he afraid of, damn it? What is there to be afraid of here?

The lifeguard taps me on the shoulder. "Sir, leave that kid alone, will you!"

This is typical. Instead of helping a father overcome the difficulties of teaching, instead of offering a cork lifebelt, instead of getting things going, this nitwit comes to the assistance of the noisy minority. I lift the eaglet out of the water and return to land, hardly concealing my scorn. My son stops on the steps and cries as he has never cried before, while I dive into the water.

I do an elegant swan dive to show the silly boy what he is missing. I use my favorite breast stroke, but something has gone wrong. It feels as if there is no coordination between my legs and my arms, as if I am sinking. Hell, what do you mean as if – I am sinking . . . Mummy! After giving just one lesson to my son, I have forgotten – forgotten how to swim.

☐ *"Don't put off until tomorrow what you can do today," the well-known enervating proverb says, and the Jewish people have adopted it without protest. Except where the payment of debts is concerned. Because in this sensitive field subconscious streams are working in an exactly opposite direction. Rumor has it that the Ten Commandments were actually eleven, the eleventh being: "Thou shalt not pay." But Aaron, Moses' brother, struck this off because, it will be remembered, he happened to be in charge of Internal Revenues.*

FUHRMAN PAYS

———◻———

On Wednesday at 5:00 P.M. I went again to see Fuhrman. I had made up my mind: this would be the last battle. This time Fuhrman would pay, or else. About four months ago Fuhrman had commissioned a publicity slogan for his factory, and to this day I had not received my fee. At first I hoped he would pay without being asked, but as this did not come to pass, I inquired politely what was the matter? Fuhrman asked me to submit a bill. I submitted a bill for Sh.95 and waited, but nothing happened.

I went to Fuhrman and we agreed to meet at the end of the week and settle the matter. We met at the end of the week. Fuhrman asked me what I wanted to discuss with him. I said: "I'd like to get my money."

"Ah," said Fuhrman, "of course." He promised to phone me soon.

Two months later I called again at his place. He asked me what could he do for me? I said: "Ninety-five shekels."

"Oh," Fuhrman said, "of course, but right now I've got terrible heartburn. Please come at the end of the week."

I said to him: "Look, Mr. Fuhrman, it's a matter of a measly ninety-five shekels."

He asked me to come back Friday morning. I came, but he was busy, so I had to wait outside. When at last he came out, I was furious.

"Tell me, Mr. Fuhrman," I accosted him, "how much longer will I have to wait for my money?"

Fuhrman threw a mean, hostile glance at me: "Come at five thirty on Wednesday."

So this was the Wednesday. I had arrived at five for fear of being preceded by some heartburn. I let myself into Fuhrman's office and, without saying a word, locked the door and pocketed the key. Fuhrman threw a glum glance at me; it was obvious he had forgotten all about me and had stayed in his office only by mistake. Frowning, he looked at his watch, then tried an anemic smile. Come to think of it, Fuhrman is not an evil man. He only hates to pay. Nobody likes to pay, but he likes it even less. His fortune is estimated between 30 and 40 millions – he owns a number of banks and forests.

"Take a seat." Fuhrman settled down in his armchair. "What can I do for you?"

I told him I had come for the 95 shekels.

"This morning I was at a funeral," said Fuhrman. "We buried poor Shmulevitz. Such a crowd came to the funeral. The old man was well liked. Did you know him?"

"No."

"I still haven't recovered from the shock. I cried like a little child. One can almost feel death's wings. . . ."

I recognized the danger in the nick of time. Now he would say we are made of dust and return to dust, it's not worth kicking up such a row for Sh.95, the Grim Reaper may gather us up any moment now. . . .

"Life goes on, Mr. Fuhrman," I whispered. "We've got to carry on with the little trials and tribulations of everyday life."

"You're right. We've got to carry on." Fuhrman sighed and rose to leave the office. But the key was in my pocket, the door locked. I again mentioned the matter of my payment. Greatly puzzled, Fuhrman asked what payment I was talking about. I explained to him that he still owed me Sh.95.

"Oh yes, now I remember," said Fuhrman. "I'll write you out a check." I asked whether I couldn't have cash. He looked at me, shocked: Sh.95 in cash? Then he started examining his calendar to see on which day I could come and fetch my check.

"No, Fuhrman," I whispered hoarsely. "Now!"

"As you like, if you insist. Cup of tea?"

"Thanks," I said, "it's too hot for tea."

Fuhrman said he needed a drink. I opened the door and, holding on to his arm, walked him to the end of the passage. Fuhrman ordered half a cup of tea. Back in the office, he complained of the tea vendor's exorbitant prices. Fuhrman has about eight factories and mines. Two supermarkets. I locked the door again and pocketed the key.

The situation was quite clear. Fuhrman was marking time in the hope that time would be working for him. Any moment now something unexpected might happen. A war, nuclear attack, earthquake, you name it.

"There were times when we made four agorot in the orange groves," Fuhrman reminisced, "and lived like kings on that."

"Will you please make out a check?"

"As you like." Fuhrman rummaged around in his pocket. The checkbook was not there. Tomorrow maybe? I reminded him that the checkbook was obviously in the desk drawer. No, no, out of the question. Yet he opened the drawer. What do you know? At least ten checkbooks. The tea vendor knocked at the door. While I let him in, Fuhrman quickly locked the drawer. As I stirred the tea, the alarming thought flashed through his mind that he had left the heartburn pills at home.

"Never mind," I said, "I've got Alka-Seltzers on me."

Fuhrman blanched. Only now did he realize that I was in earnest, that I had come prepared. He sipped his tea with furrowed brows. Poor Shmulevitz, may he rest in peace, only last week he was still sitting in this very chair. My check, please. Oh yes. But he didn't have anything to write with. I handed him my ballpoint pen. The widow was absolutely heartbroken. Most people had liked the old man.

A slight shudder runs through Fuhrman's body. He opens his checkbook. "So it's ninety shekels?"

"Ninety-five."

Fuhrman becomes pensive, he nods sadly. My pen doesn't write. He is trying, but it just won't write. So there is nothing to be done but to go home and settle it another time. I have brought another pen. Unfortunately, this one does write. So it's ninety? Ninety-five. All right, ninety-five. I can see from his trembling earlobes that he is still thinking of the late Shmulevitz. I say to him: "Please hurry up, Mr. Fuhrman, I've got to go home sometime." The first beads of sweat appear on his forehead. Fuhrman's glance skips nervously across the room. The key is in my pocket. Fuhrman writes out my name and carefully dots the i. The phone rings. What relief! Conceivably, it's one of his men hired just for this purpose. Fuhrman chats for half an hour. It's late, he says in the end. He has to leave. His brother is sick. I lift the paper knife from his desk. Fuhrman watches me keenly. Heinrich has been bedridden for the last five days. The doctor thinks it's a virus. His brother is an artist, recently returned from Mexico.

"The check, Fuhrman!"

I can feel my eyes burning. Fuhrman realizes now that the smallest tactical error could cost him his life. He rises slowly to his feet and backs away from the desk. He has a sister as well, interior decoration. A family of artists. I follow him. He goes to concerts himself. Especially Tchaikovsky, Bartók. Fuhrman moves toward the window. I quickly cut him off. Still, Beethoven is Beethoven. The Ninth. He had planned to jump out of the window and then, with a broken leg, home by taxi, quickly pack a suitcase and out to the airport. Now he is forced back to his chair. "Sign it, Fuhrman, sign the check or else your last hour has come."

He signs.

In his eyes there is a great deal of human suffering. He does not hate me or loathe me, he only despises me because of my stinginess. I feel exhausted myself. I went through a great deal during the sad days preceding the Second World War, but I can't ever remember such tension.

Before my mind's eye there appears a chart illustrating the number of calories used up by the human body: woodcutting, 2,500 calories; breaking wild horses, 4,600 calories; check from Fuhrman, 9,700 calories.

Fuhrman leafs through the calendar. It is now June. July, August, September, October, November, December, January, February – here he stops, ponders. Then writes it down: February 28. I ask him to kindly write it out for an earlier date, say January. Sorry, but that's impossible, people are not paying him either, he has to make sure the check is covered. It is a hopeless argument. Fuhrman has aged considerably in the past few hours. His cheeks sag, there are rings around his eyes. He has turned completely gray. Yesterday the papers reported that he was taking over the state-owned steel mills.

All that is left now is to write down the year on the check. With that, the check should be complete. Goodness! Fuhrman is staring at the ceiling, his bloodless lips muttering a mute prayer. The earthquake is late. 1-9-8 Fuhrman wipes his brow. Drinks from the empty teacup. Then looks deeply into my eyes. A shiver runs down my spine. Now he hates me, maniacally, eternally and irrevocably. Fuhrman grips pen number two and hovers over the check.

"Wouldn't you like to go to the theater?" he asks in a dying voice. "I've got a ticket, if you hurry you could still make it. . . ."

The paper knife points at him. Silence. Poor Shmulevitz. Tchaikovsky. End of the line. The game is over. He inserts the missing "1" to make it 1981. Finished. The pen drops out of his lifeless fingers. His face turns into a death mask. His skin is yellow, his glance bemused. I take the check. His hand stretches out listlessly and drops like a mortally wounded dove. I take my leave – "'Bye, Mr. Fuhrman, thank you very much and sorry for the disturbance. . . ."

Fuhrman does not answer, only stares at me with glassy eyes. The earth no longer revolves. Time has stopped. Fuhrman has paid.

☐ *Nothing is harder to bear than a moral debt, except a monetary debt. But a combination of the two is lethal.*

The Hardest Currency

―――□―――

As a rule I keep a supply of 50 agorot coins in my pocket. On that morning, it had run out. I stood there in front of the cruel parking meter and scratched my head. Should an inspector pass this way, the pleasure of his company would cost me Sh.50. I tried to insert a larger coin into the slot, but the meter would have none of it.

"Fifty agorot?" I suddenly heard to starboard. "Well, let's see. . . ."

I turned in the direction of the voice and beheld Glick the engineer standing on the curb, fumbling in his pocket.

"Here you are!"

With that he fed the longed-for coin to the voracious parking meter. I did not know how to thank him. I offered him the larger coin, but he would not accept it.

"Aw, come on," he said, "it's not worth mentioning!"

"Wait, I'll change it at the kiosk."

"Stop it, will you! You'll find a way to reciprocate, I'm sure."

And with that he left me with my thoughts and in a rather unpleasant situation. I don't like to be in anybody's debt. "You'll find a way" – what way? What did he mean by that? Just to be on the safe side, I stopped at the florist's on my way home and sent Mrs. Glick ten red carnations. That's how a gentleman behaves, if I'm not mistaken.

Why deny it? I expected the Glicks to give me a ring. Not that I felt special thanks were due me for the flowers, but still. . . . By nightfall there had been no call. I rang the florist. The flowers had gone by messenger at 4:30. What was going on? I could no longer stand the tension and rang the Glicks.

Glick himself came to the phone and we had a long talk about the port of Ashdod and the new government and things like that. I stood it for fifteen minutes.

"By the way," I said, "did your wife get the flowers?"

"Yes. I think Rabin should not give in to the pressure of the religious. After all, he received a clear mandate...."

And so on. I could feel my ears burning. Obviously, something had been very wrong with the flowers. When the tiresome conversation with Glick concluded, I related the whole affair to my spouse.

"But of course," the little one said with finality. "I, too, would have felt insulted. Who sends carnations nowadays? The cheapest flowers on the market."

"But I sent ten."

"Aw, stop it, you made a horrible impression. Now they'll take us for misers."

I blushed. You can call me many names, but "miser"? Next morning I went to the bookstore downstairs and bought Churchill's *History of the Second World War* in four very fat volumes indeed, and sent them to Glick the engineer.

There was no call by nightfall. The tension was well-nigh unbearable. Twice I dialed their number, but at the last moment replaced the receiver. Perhaps they did not realize that it was I who had sent the nice gift? "Impossible," the bookstore owner assured me, "I clearly wrote that it was a gift from you."

Two terrible days passed in nerve-racking silence. Then on Tuesday the books were returned with a terse note.

"Dear friend," Glick the engineer wrote, "when will you understand at long last that I don't expect any reward for the help I gave you on November 15, 1982? I did whatever I did out of good will and the desire to extend a helping hand to a fellow man in distress and that's all. I feel certain that you, too, would have acted in the same way. My reward is the wonderful feeling that I am still a human being in this jungle of selfishness and cruelty. Yours, Glick. P.S. I already have the Churchill."

I read the letter to my wife in a faltering voice.

"Of course," the little one said, "some things simply cannot be paid with money. Sometimes, believe me, a small attention outweighs the most expensive gift. But you'll never understand that, I'm afraid."

That very day I sent Glick our subscription ticket to the Philharmonic, first series.

On the night of the concert I lay in ambush at the corner of Huberman Street. Would he come? I hugged the wall and fingered the hoard of 50 agorot coins in my pocket. Yes, Glick came all right – with his wife. I went home genuinely relieved. I don't like to be in anybody's debt. For the first time in many days I could again relax. The phone rang at ten o'clock.

"We left in the middle," Glick said in a hollow voice, "the concert was awful."

"I'm desolate," I stuttered, "I'm so sorry. I wanted to reciprocate for your nice gesture...."

"Ho-ho, old boy," Glick interrupted me. "Giving is an art! Don't think twice, don't make petty calculations, give with your whole heart. Never mind what, just give! Take myself, for instance! When on that day I saw what a desperate plight you were in at the parking meter, I could well have said to myself: 'What business is this of yours! You have no car, you don't have to show solidarity with him. Pretend you never saw him and that's that!' But I'm not a designing person. 'This man needs you,' I said to myself and the purse was right there in my hand."

I could literally feel myself wilting. Why, damn it, am I totally devoid of the faculty to make a nice gesture? Never mind what, just give, give....

"Glick is one hundred percent right," the little woman opined. "You made such a mess of it that now only a dramatic step can save the situation."

We racked our brains all day long. What to do? Buy them an apartment? Shares? Appoint them my sole heirs? In the end Glick's casual remark gave us a clue. How had he put it in his long monologue? "I have no car," he had said, if memory served me.

"I don't want to be left . . . without a car," I mumbled dejectedly.

"That's typical," the wife replied. "Levantine!"

Our car was dispatched to the Glicks with two explanatory phrases: "Bon voyage," I wrote, "and thanks again."

This time their reaction was rewarding, though somewhat reserved.

"Morning," he said, "sorry to bother you, but I can't find the jack."

The blood drained out of my face. The jack had been stolen more than a year ago and I had still not bought a new one! Now Glick would have a flat tire somewhere on the road and curse me to the end of his days.

"I'm coming!" I yelled into the phone and hurried by taxi to buy a jack. I don't like to be in anybody's debt. So I drove straight to Jaffa, but suddenly on Rothschild Boulevard I came across my former car.

It was standing in front of a parking meter.

And next to the parking meter stood Glick the engineer, fumbling in his pockets.

With a hoarse shout I jumped out of the taxi and hurried over to the poor wretch.

"Fifty agorot?" I inquired. "Well, let's see. . . ."

Glick turned round, stung. Blanching, he sobbed:

"Thanks! I don't need one! I've got one! I've got one! I've got one!"

And he went on feverishly rummaging in his pockets. Both of us were breathing heavily, because we realized only too well what was at stake. With shaking hands Glick turned all his pockets inside out, but did not find even a single 50 agorot coin. I shall never forget the hunted look in his eyes. With a slow and deliberate movement I inserted a coin into the pitiless slot.

"Here you are!"

Glick aged years in a matter of minutes. His back bent, he

extracted the keys of the car and handed them over to me. He added the Philharmonic subscription, his eyes swimming in tears. By nightfall a bunch of flowers arrived for the wife. You have to hand it to Glick: he's a good loser.

□ *A Scandinavian crown prince once remarked: "To eat or not to eat," and ever since mankind has been beating out its brains over the question: to have a little something before you go to the Pomeranzes' or to put your trust in the big meal — hopefully — waiting there?*

PEANUTS FOR THE MASSES

———□———

"Ephraim, are you sure it's for dinner?"
"I think I'm sure."

I had explained to the wife a hundred times if I had explained to her once what the situation was, and yet she kept on asking. I had spoken on the phone to Mrs. Pomeranz and accepted with thanks her invitation for Wednesday at 8:30 P.M. And ever since then we'd been endlessly analyzing that conversation, because Mrs. Pomeranz hadn't said it was for dinner; on the other hand she hadn't said it wasn't.

"You don't invite people for 8:30 sharp without dinner." This was the wife's view. "Apparently it's dinner."

I thought so, too. If they don't intend to feed you, they say "don't come before eight" or else "between eight and nine" but never 8:30 sharp. Besides, I thought that Mrs. Pomeranz had particularly stressed the hour. She had said at 8:30, stressing the "at," and besides, there had been a definitely dinnerish tone in her voice.

"No, it's for dinner, I'm almost sure."

I proposed to call Mrs. Pomeranz and as if by the way ask her if she was preparing something nice, but the wife said that wouldn't be polite. Anyway, on that Wednesday we were busy all day and just had sandwiches for lunch, so that by nightfall we were quite hungry, but the wife said it was not worth eating anything at home.

"I know the Pomeranzes," she said. "If it's for dinner, we're going to get the works."

Before our mind's eye there appeared a trolley groaning with shish kebab, turkey, salads, French fries, and savories tastefully arranged. If only they wouldn't talk a lot, at least until after dinner.

We arrived at the Pomeranzes' and right away started worrying. First of all, no one else had arrived yet, and even the Pomeranzes were still dressing. Our concerned glances swept over the salon and there was not a hint of anything solid. The equipment was standard: chairs and armchairs around a low table, and on the low table a big plate of peanuts, almonds and raisins, a few olives and pieces of white cheese with plastic toothpicks sticking out of them, a cucumber, salt sticks. It flashed through my mind that maybe Mrs. Pomeranz had after all said on the phone 8:45 and not 8:30, or maybe she had not mentioned the time at all and we had only discussed Fellini's $8\frac{1}{2}$.

"What would you like to drink?"

Mr. Pomeranz came in, still tying his tie, and poured us a John Collins. This is a lovely drink, a third brandy, a third soda and a little Collins, we were always glad to drink it, but this time we were completely turkey-orientated and craving massive things. We felt a terrible emptiness in our stomachs while we clinked glasses, smiling cordially.

"*Lechaim*," Pomeranz said, and added, "What do you think of Sartre?"

I took a fistful of peanuts and tried to analyze existentialism as it affected us, but only too soon it transpired that I hadn't enough material. After all, what are a plateful of peanuts and a few almonds for a grown man? The wife was sitting under the same constellation. She had finished off the black olives at one stroke and had played havoc with the white cheese. When we came to the bombing of Colonel Gaddafi, all that was left on the low table was a lonely piece of cucumber.

"Sorry." Mrs. Pomeranz smiled, with raised eyebrows. "I'll get some more."

She took the devastated plates to the kitchen. As she opened the door, we tried to catch a glimpse of the kitchen, hoping against hope that some unusual preparations were going on there, but the results were literally frightening. The kitchen looked completely sterile, the atmosphere alarmingly calm. In the meantime several more guests had arrived — at 9:15 (?) — and my stomach suddenly let out such a fearful screech of anguish that I almost died of shame. I silenced it with a second plate of peanuts, and then began to feel slightly sick. Not that I had anything against peanuts — quite the contrary. Peanuts are very nutritious food with a lot of proteins, only they can't serve as ersatz for turkey, bread and fish salad with mayonnaise.

I looked up. The little woman, chalk-white, was gripping her throat; it was obvious that the cucumbers and the raisins were fighting the John Collins inside her. I threw myself on a fresh cargo of white cheese and I think I also swallowed a toothpick. I simply couldn't stop. Mrs. Pomeranz looked at us askance, then exchanged a few words with her husband and returned to the kitchen to replenish her stocks.

"*Nu*," someone remarked at my elbow, "the number of unemployed is growing day by day."

"Of course," I answered, "the government is starving us."

I could hardly speak because of the salt sticks in my mouth. As a matter of fact, why did I have to listen to this crap about unemployment when here in the middle of the salon a whole family was dying for a piece of bread? The little wife finished off the third lot of peanuts, and the first traces of panic appeared on the faces of our hosts. Pomeranz took out of a cupboard some toffees, which quickly joined the rest of the victuals. Remember, we had had hardly a thing since the morning. The salt sticks were setting up such a racket in my mouth that they deafened me from inside. The skin was drum-tight on my belly and I felt slightly dizzy. At a conservative estimate, I had swallowed about four pounds of peanuts, several tins of sticks and a sea of salt. I had long ago lost any trace of self-control. I kept hiccupping and groaning and had all sorts of psychedelic visions. The little woman had turned into a chunk of toffee and her eyes were imploring mutely. Mr. Pomeranz brought some olives from the neighbors'. I had reached a stage where the very thought of peanuts caused me unspeakable nausea. Let's not think of food. Let's not think of any food at all.

"Ladies and gentlemen, please come in!"

Pomeranz opened the door of the next room and before our eyes there appeared a big table with a snow-white cloth . . . plates . . . glasses . . . Good Lord!

Mrs. Pomeranz rolled in a trolley loaded with turkey, mushroom soup, French fries, asparagus, salads. . . .

"Please be seated."

The rest I don't remember.

The Economics of Baby-Sitting

———□———

I think it is quite superfluous to introduce Regina Fleischhacker. By common consent, she is the best-qualified baby sitter in the National League, a real pearl: punctual, loyal, soft-spoken, a wizard with the diapers. Baby Amir has never yet had reason to complain of her. There is only one flaw in Mrs. Fleischhacker's otherwise consummate perfection: she lives in Tel Giborim, in the heart of the Holon wilderness, and therefore has no direct connection with our place. She has to travel by *sherut* or shuttle-taxi to the Central Bus Station and there switch to another sherut, and sometimes there is no sherut and she has to squeeze her bulk into a jam-packed, slow-motion bus, and on such occasions she arrives in a state of near collapse, her eyes full of mute reproach.

"Again, no sherut."

So around 8:00 P.M. we always start praying that there will be a sherut and sometimes it helps. But we are terribly anxious about the future, because there is no substitute for Regina Fleischhacker. If only she would not live in Tel Giborim, without a phone.

What is this long introduction leading up to?

Well, it leads up to a certain evening when we planned to leave at 8:30 for the late show. On that same evening at sundown I had started writing a series of personal and most urgent letters, and because of the humidity my style did not flow as smoothly as it should have. At 8:30 the seasoned baby sitter arrived and her eyes clearly told us that again there had been no sherut.

"I ran," she panted, "I ran like a madwoman."

In such cases, the correct and tactful thing to do is storm out of the house, in order to justify the mad baby sitter's marathon dash. But, as I said, the urgent letters were not yet finished. And, indeed, a few

THE ECONOMICS OF BABY-SITTING

minutes later the door of my study flew open.

"You are still here?"

"Just a second...."

"Then why must I run like a madwoman, if you have all the time in the world?"

"We're ... we're ready."

"Why call me at all if you're staying home?"

"We'll pay ... even if...."

"No need to pay, ma'am!" said Regina Fleischhacker majestically. "I don't take money for the time I don't work! Next time kindly think twice before you call me!"

Without further ado I grabbed my typewriter and we fled out of the house. I finished the letters at the pastry shop across the street. The typing caused a mild sensation, but gradually people became accustomed to it.

Naturally, we did not make it to the cinema that night. My little wife, that born Realpolitiker, proposed that we kill the three-hour minimum of the professional baby sitter by strolling in the city streets. Tel Aviv is beautiful at night. Especially on the seashore, the northern suburbs, Jaffa and the Abu Kabir Plain. We returned at midnight on our last legs and paid the prescribed Sh.36.

"When will you be needing me again?" Regina asked, her eyebrows raised.

The little woman looked at me, expecting a snap decision. Yet any mistake would have been fatal because Mrs. Fleischhacker has no phone, so that a date once made cannot be canceled. She lived in Tel Giborim, remember, and lacked direct communications.

"Day after tomorrow? At eight?"

"All right," I mumbled. "I think ... we'll go to the movies."

Hidden are the ways of the Almighty.

On that day after tomorrow, at 7:00 P.M., my back started aching something awful. I think I even ran a temperature. My faithful wife stood at my bedside, greatly concerned.

"You've got to get up." She snapped her fingers. "She'll be here any moment now and we've got to go."

"But I'm sick!"

"Make an effort, for goodness' sake! It will be terribly embarrassing if she sees that she came all the way from Tel Giborim for nothing again."

"I'm dizzy."

"So am I. Take an aspirin. Come on, get up."

Regina, that walking Swiss chronometer, arrived at eight sharp, breathing heavily.

"Shalom," she hissed, "again there was no...."

I dressed in panic. If there had been a sherut, we might conceivably have started negotiations, but like this, what with buses and all, organized resistance was out of the question. We left in a hurry. Outside, I fell against the wall, too weak to stand. I felt really lousy – it must have been flu or something. What was to be done? The cinema was out of the question in such a state.

We got into our car and I stretched out on the rear seat. I'm rather tall and our car is small. "O Lord," I wailed, "why do I have to crouch here in our car with the grippe almost killing me, why?" The Lord did not answer my query and besides I am also blessed with a tinge of claustrophobia. The crisis drew to a head seventy-five minutes later.

"Woman," I whispered, "I'm turning in."

"Already?" the little one exclaimed in the car's clammy darkness. "Only an hour and a half. Do you expect her to come all the way from Tel Giborim for so little?"

"I don't expect her to do anything," I croaked. "Only I don't want to die for Mrs. Fleischhacker. I'm still young, life is beautiful. I'm turning in, woman."

"Come on, wait another twenty minutes."

"I can't."

"You know what?" the little one caught up with me in front of the entrance. "Let's try and slip in without her hearing us. We'll sit quietly in our bedroom and wait."

THE ECONOMICS OF BABY-SITTING

That sounded reasonable. I agreed. We opened the door slowly and tiptoed in. A shaft of light came from my study. So that's where the Fleischhacker was. We advanced cautiously, taking advantage of every irregularity in the well-known terrain, but a few steps before the objective, misfortune struck.

"Who's there?" Regina roared from my study. "Who goes there?"

We turned on the light.

"It's us," the wife quickly called out. "Ephraim forgot the present."

What present? The wife threw me a menacing glance, walked up to the bookshelf and after hesitating for just the fraction of a second, pulled out the *History of the English Theater, 1616–1985*. Then we said "Sorry" and exited with the book. In front of the door I felt faint, and for the first time red polka dots appeared before my eyes. One of my molars also started hurting. I sat down on the curb and, if memory serves me, started sobbing.

"It was our only chance." The wife passed her cool hand over my burning brow. "In an hour or two we'll be able to turn in."

"If I survive," I took an oath, "we'll move to Tel Giborim, across the street from Mrs. Fleischhacker."

Half an hour later I informed my wife that I was ready for another try.

This time it worked.

Our previous experience in self-infiltration stood us in good stead. The door fell shut with the lightest of clicks. The light in the study was still burning bright. We made the bedroom according to plan, closed the sliding doors with feeling, stretched out on our beds and waited for the three hours to pass.

As to what happened next, there is a certain gap in my memory.

"Ephraim," I suddenly heard my little wife's voice as from a distance, "it's five-thirty!"

She shook me with all her might. I blinked in the strong light coming through the windows. It had been a long time since I had enjoyed such refreshing sleep. Our strategic position, on the other hand, was deplorable.

"We've got to get Regina out of there," the little one mused. "Wait...."

With that she went out and slipped into Amir's adjacent room. Two tense seconds later the baby's high-frequency yells almost cracked the walls. The wife sprinted back.

"Did you pinch him?"

"Of course."

Regina Fleischhacker's heavy body hurtled toward the nursery like a flash. We took advantage of the commotion, made for the front door, went out and came back through it, calling loudly: "Good morning!"

"Is this a time to come home?" a bleary-eyed Regina asked, cradling an angry Amir in her arms. "Where have you been?"

"At an orgy."

"Today's youth!" Regina shook her head and presented the bill. Then she stepped out into the cool morning to look for a sherut to Tel Giborim. I bet you she didn't find one.

☐ *What's the difference between the plumber and the Messiah? The Messiah might yet show up, but the Hebrew plumber never comes, unless he is forced at gunpoint. The fate of our dripping faucets depends on who is quicker on the draw.*

THE PLUMBER

—☐—

Some afternoons ago the innards of our kitchen tap burst and the water poured out of it with elemental force. I immediately went to the only plumber of the neighborhood, a certain Stucks, intending to ask him to the sick tap's bedside. Only his wife was at home, but she said he would come to my place around noon. I waited for a while, but he did not come, so I went there again. Only his wife was at home and she said that though her husband had been home in the meantime, he could not come yet, as he had to go somewhere else. He would come to my place before the evening.

Stucks did not come in the evening, so I went to him, but there was nobody at home. The neighbors said maybe the Stuckses had gone to the cinema, they did not know for sure. I left a note in the keyhole saying would Mr. Stucks please come in the morning because the tap was leaking badly.

Stucks did not come in the morning, so I went to his place and nabbed him just as he was about to go out. He said he was on his way to me, but now that we had met, perhaps I would agree that he shouldn't come till noon, because he had to go to the Municipality. He said he would come around one; I asked him if we could not move it to half past one, as this would be more convenient for me, but he said he was sorry, it was out of the question, it would have to be either one or not at all.

I waited until 3:00 P.M., but he did not come, so I went to his place. Only his wife was at home, but she said she would intercede with her husband on my behalf. I asked Mrs. Stucks when she thought he could come, and she answered as soon as he came home – right now he was working at the factory because the foreman was sick.

I waited at home for about two hours, but Stucks did not show up, so I went to his place. Stucks was just having his lunch and said he had not been able to come because he had been busy all the time, but now he would just take a few bites and be with me in no time at all.

I waited until the evening, but he did not come, so I went to his place, but there was nobody at home. I sat down on the doorstep and waited for them to come home, but they didn't come until midnight. I asked Stucks why had he not come to repair the tap, so he said he had been busy up to now, but I had nothing to worry about, he would come without fail at half past seven in the morning. I asked him if he could not come at seven, but he said no, that was out of the question. In the end we settled on 7:15.

I waited until ten, but he did not come, so I went to his place. Only his wife was at home and she promised to remind her husband to come as soon as he returned. When I left she ran after me and asked who I was and what I wanted. I told her that the tap was leaking badly, could Mr. Stucks come at once? If he had promised to come, the woman said, he would certainly come. He had not come by noon, so I went to his place. He was just having his lunch and said he would just swallow a few bites and come.

"You know what?" I said. "I'll wait for you." Whereupon Stucks calmly finished a very substantial meal, rose, yawning, and said he was sorry, but he always had to take a nap after lunch, then went to the adjoining room. I waited in my chair until seven in the evening, when Mrs. Stucks said, oh yes, her husband had left long ago through the kitchen. But she would tell him when he came home that I had waited for him.

What's the use of all this running hither and thither? I decided to sit it out then and there. Stucks came home at nine and said he was sorry, but because of the weather he had completely forgotten about me. What was it that I wanted? Look, I said, if you don't want to come, say so. I'll go to somebody else to have the tap repaired. There are other plumbers in the neighborhood. "But why shouldn't I come?" Stucks said. "That's what I do for a living." He even gave his word of honor that he would come at seven sharp in the morning. One night more would make no difference.

Instinct took me to his door at 5:00 A.M. He was just setting out for the city with long, vigorous steps: he was on army reserve duty that day. Wait, I said, and joined him.

In camp I did not let him out of my sight for a moment. We trained together on difficult terrain, dismantled a few mines, then on the way home he said, excuse me, I'll just change into overalls and come.

I waited for a while, but he did not come, so I went to his place, but only his wife was at home, and she promised to tell him that I had been looking for him. He did not come in the evening, so I bought a slightly used pistol and went on waiting for Stucks until noon. Stucks came home, then lay down for his customary nap. I asked him whether he would object if I handcuffed his left arm to my wrist. He said, go right ahead.

We slept for about half an hour, then set out for my place. On the way Stucks unexpectedly pulled his arm out of the handcuff and started running. I fired a burst at him. He returned fire, then ran out of ammunition, came out with raised hands, and repaired the tap.

This morning it started dripping again.

☐ *Our sympathy for elephants stems from the fact that, as a small and fighting nation, we instinctively side with the underdog. This historic sympathy of ours is subject to only one reservation: the underdog must be house-trained.*

TSVINJI PEES

Tsvinji, the Curse of the Mongolian Steppes, was discovered one cold dawn in what, at the time, still qualified as my ornamental garden. It was about 5:30 A.M. and people were still a-slumber, all except politicians, who have to get up early lest the wheels stop turning. Suddenly a desperate whine filtered in through the Venetian blinds. Bleary-eyed, I raised a blind and peered out. In the middle of my now defunct ornamental garden a very small puppy was digging up the ground with his little paws and chewing up the greenery around him – toothless, but with great gusto. The puppy was very white, very young, of indeterminate race, and quite incapable of coordinating the movement of its four legs. I was just about to close the blind and return to my warm blankets, but then my wife spoke up.

"What's that?"

"A puppy."

"How cute," she said. "Show me."

I opened the door wide, whereupon the puppy tottered into our room and peed on the red carpet.

I don't like having my red carpet peed on. So I grabbed the puppy and removed him to the garden in the hope that He who nourishes the birds of the sky would also remove him somewhere. But the puppy turned on a shrill whine, whereupon our neighbor Mrs. Toscanini rushed over to us in her dressing gown and embarked on a formal speech in favor of our adopting the little orphan. She dwelt on the well-known fact that a dog is a faithful animal, and clever too, and clean; as a matter of fact, man has no better friend in this rotten world, except the Government, maybe.

"All right," I said to Mrs. Toscanini, "if it's so desirable to keep a dog, why don't you adopt this one?"

"Do you think I'm out of my mind?" said Mrs. Toscanini. "Haven't I got enough troubles?"

And that's how the puppy was adopted by us. After a brief family confab, we gave him the brand-new name of Tsvinji, because of the brown spots on his ears, or perhaps for some other reason I don't quite remember. Tsvinji quickly attained member-of-the-family status and gradually wormed himself into our hearts. In all fairness, one has to admit that he ate anything that came within range of his jaws, from radio aerials to alarm clocks; he also carried home from the neighboring gardens all sorts of little cadavers. On the other hand, the little mutt was very much attached to us and wagged his tail like a metronome whenever we called him, provided he spotted Hungarian salami in our hands. Within an amazingly brief time I taught Tsvinji a large number of commands – to quote but a few: "Down! Down!" (Tsvinji cocks his ears and licks my face), and "Jump!" (at this command Tsvinji as a rule scratches his belly), and "Paw!" (the dog does not move, plays possum). In short, Tsvinji is not one of those trained, servile dogs that obey orders mechanically, but an independent, clever, adult canine.

But he always pees on the carpet.

He always pees and only on the carpet.

Why?

We don't know. According to the basic laws of psychology, it may be assumed that this is a result of certain experiences in the suckling period. In other words, Tsvinji was born in a field of red poppies, and therefore whenever he sees the red carpet for which I paid a fortune, he has got to pee or it's the end of the world.

But, as a matter of fact, the reason is not important – the facts and the stains remain facts and stains.

Naturally, I did not resign myself to Tzvinji's curious habits, and after a few weeks I started him on a severe withdrawal regime.

"It's forbidden on the carpet! Forbidden! Phooey!" I shouted at him whenever he favored the red carpet with his attentions. On the other hand, I lavished praise and caresses on him whenever he fulfilled his needs by mistake in my ornamental garden, though under the impact of his growing teeth the garden gradually took on the look of the Gobi Desert. From all these actions of mine Tsvinji drew the conclusion that I am a very capricious god who alternately rages and radiates happiness because of his peeing – who can understand these humans?

Personally, I had to admit that Tsvinji was simply unable to grasp the most elementary rules of hygiene and therefore I decided to break him of this childish habit gradually. My plan was that first I'd accustom him to peeing not on red but on other carpets; then gradually I'd lure him outdoors, so that he could unburden himself there – or, even better, on neighboring land. With that aim in view, I covered the red carpet with a gray one and fixed half a bottle of cream as reward for every peeing carried out on a gray background. A week later, when Tsvinji had obviously become accustomed to gray, I unveiled the red carpet again, whereupon the cur made a mad dash for it (faithfulness!) and was happier than ever before.

Then I introduced an exercise routine designed to inculcate a love of nature in Tsvinji's heart. I bought a strong green leash and every night walked the animal to Petach Tikva and back. All through our walk Tsvinji gave proof of remarkable restraint, but as we approached our home he became restless and from the doorway made a beeline for the red carpet.

I understood that this was due to a complicated biological process which probably had deep roots, but occasionally the thought flashed through my mind: why should I put up with it? I mentioned this to the wife and she said that she was a follower of Rousseau, the French philosopher, who had stated that anything that was natural was beautiful. In other words, it was natural that Tsvinji should always pee on our red carpet.

But what does nature do in its boundless wisdom?

One morning Mrs. Toscanini came over to donate some bones for the dog and I complained to her that the dog was all mixed up hygiene-wise.

"Because you don't know how to educate him," Mrs. Toscanini said. "What you have to do is this: every time he wets the red carpet, rub his nose in the puddle, slap his rump and toss him out the window. That's how it's done."

That's what I did, although I'm not an advocate of corporal punishment. Tsvinji came, did, I rubbed his nose, slapped him and tossed him out the window. Breaking Tsvinji's habit had become my life's vocation. If the process had to be repeated three times, I repeated it three times. And slowly, gradually, I achieved some results. Nowadays Tsvinji no longer behaves as of old. Something of training has stuck. True, he still pees only on the red carpet, but afterwards he jumps out of the window all by himself without any assistance from me. Then he waits outside for me to come and praise him.

☐ *"Love thy neighbor as thyself," the absurd Hebrew commandment goes, meaning you shouldn't do to your fellow man what you wouldn't have him do to you. A nice law, universally respected. In any case, on the strength of this law, never give a loan to your friends, good people, because clearly you wouldn't like to owe money to anyone, would you?*

The Insult and the Injury

———☐———

SEPTEMBER 7. Today I ran into Adalbert Toscanini in the Passage. He looked extremely upset. It seems that he had asked Bialazurkevitz to lend him Sh. 100 just for a few days and that skunk, that monster, that heel, that rabid dog was not ashamed to say to him: "I've got them, but you can't have them!"

So that's how low we have sunk! There is not a shred of common decency left in this rotten world. "Yes, there is," I said, and there and then handed over the wretched Sh. 100 to Toscanini. "At last a human being," Adalbert whispered, choking back his tears. "I'll return them within a fortnight, rest assured."

According to the wife, I am an idiot. I explained to her: "I didn't want to make an enemy of Toscanini."

SEPTEMBER 18. Ran into Adalbert on Allenby Road. We walked side by side for a few steps and I meticulously avoided mentioning the loan. But Toscanini lost his temper and hissed at me: "Don't lose any sleep, you'll get your money back, down to the last agora! I promised to repay you within two weeks, the two weeks are not yet over, so what the hell do you want?" I told him it really was not worth getting upset over such a trifle, whereupon Toscanini remarked that I was no better than the rest and turned his back on me.

OCTOBER 3. A very painful incident at the Rio Café. Adalbert Toscanini was sitting at one of the tables with Bialazurkevitz and did not take his eyes off me for a second. He was visibly seething with anger. I tried to look pleasant, but this only added fuel to the fire. After a while Adalbert got up from his table and strode over to me: "Grossartig!" he shouted, so that everybody heard him. "So I am a few days late repaying. Is that the end of the world? Don't look at me as if I were a murderer!" I said "God forbid," whereupon he answered something rude which does not bear printer's ink. I think there are going to be complications. The wife warned me: "Didn't I tell you? You'll see, there's going to be violence.

OCTOBER 11. According to reliable information reaching me, Toscanini is spreading rumors all over the city to the effect that I am a hopeless drug addict, and that two well-known female lawyers have started paternity suits against me. Needless to say, there is not a shred of truth in all this. I don't even smoke. All the same, the wife opines that for the sake of my mental peace I ought to waive those Sh.100.

OCTOBER 14. Today I met Adalbert in the queue at the movies. His face was livid. His eyes burned red in their sockets. His neck muscles were unnaturally taut. "Look, Adalbert," I said to him good-naturedly, "in view of the difficult economic situation, let's forget about that money. Is that all right?" Toscanini flared up: "Forget nothing," he roared. "I don't need your generosity! What do you take me for – a dishrag?" I have never seen him so upset. Bialazurkevitz, with whom he was going to the cinema, had to hold him, otherwise he would have thrown himself on me. I ran straight home. The little one: "Didn't I tell you so?"

OCTOBER 29. Several people today asked me whether it was true that I had signed up with the Red Guards but had been rejected as a weakling. An utter fabrication, of course. I know only too well who is behind these rumors. Last week my windows were pelted with anonymous rocks. The whole city is talking about the life-and-death struggle going on between Toscanini and myself. Two days ago, as I came into the Rio, Toscanini jumped up and started shouting: "May anyone come in here? What is this, a refuge for bums?" The owner pushed me out of the door, to avoid unpleasantness. "Dirty miser!" Adalbert blazed after me. "Bloodsucker!" The wife had foretold as much.

NOVEMBER 8. Today Aladar, my favorite cousin, called on us and asked me to lend him just Sh.10. "I've got them, but you can't have them!" I said to him. "Get out!" I like the boy and don't want to spoil our friendship. I've got enough trouble as it is with the Ministry of the Interior. Someone denounced me, saying I have an Aryan grandmother, and they took away my passport. So much for my plan to flee abroad. The wife, whose warning it will be remembered I had ignored, does not let me go outdoors by myself.

I went to see a psychiatrist. "Because of his strong feeling of guilt, Adalbert Toscanini hates you, sir," he explained. "A typical father complex which can be relieved only by the proverbial patricide, as a sort of conciliatory offering. A very clear case." I pointed out to him that I was still young, full of vitality. The psychiatrist informed me that Toscanini's all-consuming, mortal hatred would go on burning bright for as long as his loan still stood – that is, as long as he is unable to repay it. "Couldn't you send him some money anonymously?" I rushed to the bank, withdrew Sh.500 and dropped them into Toscanini's mailbox.

NOVEMBER 11. Today I met Adalbert on Allenby Road. He spat on the ground and walked on. I reported to the psychiatrist. "Well," he said, "we tried, we failed." From a most reliable source I learned that Adalbert has bought a doll bearing a striking resemblance to me and is now sticking pins into it every morning. The police won't intervene. Pinpricks in my back.

NOVEMBER 20. Shouts outside last night. "O Lord," I prayed on my bed of pain, "I have erred horribly, I lent money to a pal in Israel! Will I have to bear the terrible consequences of my madness to the end of my days? Is there no way out of my predicament?" I heard a deep, fatherly voice coming from above: "None."

DECEMBER 1. Pinpricks have spread to chest as well. Leaning heavily on my wife, I dragged my sick body, that victim of the father complex, to a reputable doctor. At the corner we bumped into Bialazurkevitz. "Ephraim," the wife whispered, "he is an ideal father figure. Look at his head, a typical father head." A faint glimmer of hope.

DECEMBER 3. I accosted Toscanini in front of the Rio. "Thanks for the money," I quickly said to him before he could knock me down. "Bialazurkevitz has paid me your whole debt. True, he asked me not to tell you, but I think you deserve to know what a friend you have. So from now on, it's not to me you owe that money, but to Bialazurkevitz." Adalbert's hard face relaxed: "Bialazurkevitz is a real pal," he whispered, choking back the tears. "I'll repay him in a few days."

I am saved!

JANUARY 22. As we walked arm in arm through the Passage, Adalbert said to me: "Bialazurkevitz, that rabid dog, has been looking at me these last few days in such a way that I could slap his face. True, I owe him money, but that does not yet make me his dishrag. His little game is going to have a very sad ending!"

But that is no longer my business.

HAIR

———□———

The barbershop I patronize is perhaps not the most luxurious on the Mediterranean littoral, but it has everything needed for a ful haircut: three chairs, three basins and a bell that tinkles every time somebody opens the door. When I first caused the bell to ring, I was received by a senior tonsorial artist sporting a bald pate who pointed to an empty chair and said, "Please."

I put myself in his hands, but not before warning him that all I wanted was a trim, since I like my hair long and silky. The man nodded understandingly, and fifteen minutes later I looked like a Marine just out of boot camp. The barber's feet were treading my mutilated locks, his face glowing with the satisfaction of a job well done. The massacre over, the bald barber intimated that he was not the boss, pocketed the tip and we parted company. I did not really bear him a grudge since it was clear that the radical shearing had been prompted by an irresistible psychological urge. It was also obvious that his name was Grinshpan.

About two months later, when I had regained some of my human aspect, I again called at the barbershop. This time Grinshpan was busy curling the hair of a politician, but another barber, a skinny and heavily bespectacled man, stood next to an empty chair and said, "Please."

Right away I decided not to experiment with him but to entrust myself again to Grinshpan the Bald. True, I mused, he was a shlemiel, but by now I knew his complexes and could neutralize them. Therefore I replied to the skinny barber, "Thank you, but I'll wait for your friend here."

The skinny one grinned cordially and tucked a towel into my collar right down to my hips.

"As I said," I repeated, "I'll wait for your friend."

"Yes," the skinny one said and bade me sit down. "O.K."

Grinshpan enlightened me: "He's a new immigrant," he whispered. "Doesn't speak Hebrew."

·HAIR·

Then and there my resistance evaporated, since this was now a matter of immigrant absorption and the melting pot, and I am certainly the last person to hurt the little artisan just because he is an alien. So I surrendered to the skinny fellow and tried to explain to him in basic Rumanian that I liked a flowing mane, since I have beautiful hair, so it should not be shorn, only clipped of its unruly tips. The immigrant barber listened attentively. To my great regret he hailed from Poland. As a result of this geographic mishap, my head was quite unnecessarily shampooed and a torrent of eau de cologne poured on me. I certainly would never have taken half this punishment from a veteran barber, but, as I said, Taddeus was a new immigrant and would have interpreted any criticism on my part as something akin to kicking a man who is down.

The third round started auspiciously.

As I rung myself in I saw that the new immigrant was busy parting the hair of an anonymous patriarch, while reliable Grinshpan was free as a bird. I quicky settled down in his chair, but just then Grinshpan slipped out of his white coat and said, "Enough!" He was replaced in the mirror by a brand-new personality: the third barber, young and Oriental, called Mashiah, as I later discovered.

"Please," Mashiah said. "Haircut, sir?"

The question of balance arose. As a matter of fact, I would have preferred Immigrant Taddeus to the Third Man since he had already proved himself a taciturn worker, but in the circumstances my refusal would rightly have been interpreted as bias against the Oriental community. I looked at Grinshpan for a stop-gap solution, but he had immersed himself in an evening paper, as if to say, "This is a cruel world, sir. Every man for himself." I realized then that although Grinshpan was accepting payment for services rendered, he had no legislative authority in the shop.

"I'm into long hair," I said to Mashiah. "Please cut it with feeling."

"All right, boss," Mashiah answered, and while relating his personal story, as well as highlights from modern Moroccan history, he left more hair on my head than any hick barber I had encountered in the past eight years. It was a pleasant surprise.

Early in April I came again, but realized right away that I was in a most dangerous situation. I found that although Grinshpan was busy working up a bouffant hair-do on a midget hooligan, newcomers Taddeus and Mashiah were idle and looking for prey. I wanted to turn on my heel, so as to avoid a direct confrontation between them, but I was too late. Both of them rose and pointed to their chairs.

"Please."

It was a situation of unmatched tension, almost defying solution from the humanistic point of view, an eternal dilemma where one of them was destined to cut my hair while the other was left no choice but to throw himself on his sword.

I chose Mashiah.

The moment I sat down on his high chair I regretted my choice bitterly. Seeing that I had chosen the Orient, Taddeus winced as if he had been horsewhipped, although I assume that he had never heard that word. He quietly turned and made for the ladies' section. A little while later we heard muted sobs. I pretended not to hear, but it was an awful feeling. Now Taddeus would go home and his starving children and would cluster around him.

"*Papo, dlaczego placzesz?*"

And Taddeus would answer them: "He . . . chose . . . him. . . ."

Mashiah, too, was edgy and clipped my hair to the limits of utter baldness.

After this incident, I waited impatiently for my hair to grow, because I wanted with all my heart to compensate Taddeus for the stinging insult he had suffered. Before ringing myself in, I therefore passed the glass door several times and did not enter until I was absolutely certain that only Taddeus was free. I dashed in and made for the new immigrant's vacant chair – but inside it a minimal kid had been hiding, and this brat upped and took Taddeus' chair right from under my nose.

Mashiah stropped his razor with slow, suggestive motions, never taking his eyes off me, while Taddeus seemed to shrink and was visibly stiff under the effect of his erstwhile humiliation. Grinshpan, that snake, pretended to be quite unconcerned.

I waited on the bench panic-stricken. Who would finish first, Mashiah or Taddeus?

Should Mashiah again win me, it would be the end of the new immigrant, there was no doubt about that. It is rumored that at the Santa Catherina monastery there is a monk who once was a successful barber in Jaffa.

In the end Morocco won by a hair's breadth. The kid in Taddeus' chair still had a few hairs on the top by the time Mashiah had finished his customer.

"Sir," he summoned me, "please."

I summoned all my courage and gestured toward Taddeus, "Thanks, I'll wait for him to finish."

Taddeus' face lit up with unexpected happiness, while Mashiah tottered and grabbed the back of the chair for support. His eyes fluttered like a bird whose heart has been transfixed by an arrow.

"But," the poor fellow stuttered, "but I have finished, sir. What's the matter?"

Then Taddeus released the kid. We were left alone in the barbershop.

Quite a predicament.

Never before had I so clearly felt that man was a hapless puppet in the hands of fate. Quite possibly all this might end in murder, and nobody would be to blame, just as in a Greek tragedy. Tension rose to a peak. The new immigrant's lips worked convulsively, his nose twitching. If I took as much as another step toward Mashiah's chair, Taddeus would collapse.

Mashiah scorched me with his glance, the unsheathed razor trembling in his hand. He was suffering deeply. Grinshpan was counting money in the silence, his back turned toward us, but I noticed that his shoulders were shaking. His indifference was simply a mask. He had loved me all this time but had not shown it. A misplaced obduracy.

A strange weakness gripped me.

"You decide," I mumbled, "among yourselves."

But they didn't move. Only Grinshpan stretched his arm backward and with a slow motion turned on the hot water tap. Three pairs of staring eyes said, "Take me."

It was compromise time. Perhaps they could cut my hair as a team. Or perhaps we should play a sort of Russian roulette – one would cut my hair and the rest commit suicide. Anything to break this awful, mute tension.

We stood motionless for about twenty minutes. Or maybe half an hour. Taddeus was weeping.

"Well," I whispered, "can't you make up your minds?"

"It makes no difference," Mashiah answered hoarsely. "You take your choice, sir."

And they went on staring. I stepped up to the mirror and passed my hand over my white hair. In a matter of minutes I had aged weeks and no solution was in sight. I burst out of the barbershop without uttering another word. I have never been back. Since them I have been wearing it long. Who knows, perhaps that's how the long-haired movement started, in a barbershop with three barbers.

The Joys of Family Transport

Here, at this point, I would like to say that, everything considered, I'm still in favor of marriage. I mean, you work like a slave but you know what *for*; you gradually accumulate a houseful of smart kids, you no longer waste your precious time on every doll, chick, and cutie – in short, you've come a long way from the lone, wretched creature you were in your happy bachelor days. For what does a man crave, after all? He craves for a woman to share life's burden with, someone he can tell his troubles to. So he marries, and from then on he's got something to tell.

The particular troubles of this writer have to do with travels in the bosom of his family. The way things are I can drive my own car no more than a dozen yards before the little woman gives a loud shriek, thus: "Red! *Red!*" Or "Watch that bike! *Watch that bike!*"

These sidelong messages invariably come in pairs, the first with a big exclamation mark, the second in italics. Long ago I used to remind my wife sometimes that I hadn't a single traffic offence against me, that I'd been driving cars practically since childhood, that I had the same number of eyes she had, maybe more, and that I could therefore get along very well without her italics.

About ten years ago, however, I gave it up. I decided it wasn't a question of logic but a purely emotional matter, like the Arabs' hostility towards us. The little woman has four penalty points for traffic offences herself, but with us the points system does not operate.

Sometimes we're driving along a perfectly quiet street and suddenly the little one yells in my ear: "Ephraim! *Ephraim!*"

In a flash I turn the wheel, mount the sidewalk, hit a couple of ashcans, and crash into the steel shutters of an anonymous laundry. I switch off what's left of the engine and look around me, and there's not a living soul in sight, not one accident-prone vehicle anywhere. This street is as deserted as the Sahara.

"So why did you scream?" I ask my wife curiously. *"Why did you scream?"*

"You weren't concentrating." And she adds with a groan: "The way *you* drive! *The way* you *drive!*" and pointedly fastens her seat belt.

The kids side with Mummy, of course. The first animal my daughter Renana learnt to recognize was a zebra crossing. *A zebra crossing!* Her grandfather, too, likes to point out that I drive like a nut, *a nut.* The other day he took me aside and told me as man to man: "Look, my boy, you've got your worries and all, why not let my daughter do the driving?"

Even the kids have learnt to declare in chorus from the back seat: "Daddy, let Mummy. . . ."

They keep sending me to all sorts of courses, and shatter my pride in other more subtle ways too. I've noticed that whenever I come home from work Amir calls out: "It's only Daddy. Nothing's happened."

Why should anything have happened? And why *only* Daddy? Their four-point mother positively eggs them on. On every family drive she hisses: "Ooh, will I be happy if a cop catches you now, *Ooh, will I be happy!*" Or "That'll cost you your license, *that'll cost you your license!*"

She can only relax, according to her, when she's at the wheel herself. As often as not she takes it away from me by force with a lot of drama and hysterics and to loud applause from the gallery. To date she's twice smashed into a truck and once into a piano, has felled a parking meter and run over countless cats. Four points.

"That," she explains after every accident, "is because I'm all flustered from your wild driving. . . ."

Lately, even Max our dog has joined in the conspiracy like the bitch she is. At every sharp turn she sticks her head through the window and lets out two sharp barks: "Bow! *Wow!*" My wife says she means I should keep *both* hands on the wheel like everybody else.

Sometimes I get my bawling out ex post facto. After I've sailed

THE JOYS OF FAMILY TRANSPORT

smoothly and hitchlessly past a couple of peaceful pedestrians, the little woman asks in a voice dripping with irony: "Did you see them? *Did you even see them?*"

Sure I saw them. *Sure I saw them.* Otherwise I'd have hit them, no?

"What're you doing, for heaven's sake, *what're you doing?*"

"Thirty mph."

"You want to end up in hospital? *In hospital?*"

Her cruising speed is 75 mph., which is just about the rate of her running commentary, too. Last month she appropriated the car and whizzed off to the supermarket for some cheese. On the way, a traffic light drove into her head on and turned the car into a recoilless accordion. The little one got out from under, pale but unshaken, though for weeks afterwards her accusing look followed me wherever I went.

"Imagine, you poor thing," the look said, "what would have happened had *you* been at the wheel, God forbid!"

She has four points, as mentioned.

After several garage-bound weeks, the car has unfortunately returned to the bosom of our family. My driving has improved a lot, although ever since I have adopted the do-it-yourself method. It's sort of like preventive driving: I myself warn myself at every crossing in order to set the mind of my worried family at rest in advance.

"A stop sign in front of me!" I announce loud and clear while doing 20 mph. "*A stop sign in front of me!*" Or "Not at amber, Ephraim, *not at amber!*" And after taking a turn I mumble to myself: "The way I drive! *The way I drive!*"

At least I've got peace in my car now. The wife sits tight-lipped, the kids despise me in silence, the dog barks twice, and I drive me slowly out of my mind.

□ *During thousands of years of exile and persecution, Jewry locked itself in an intellectual ivory tower and neglected to develop its body. Our renewed country restored to Jewry the simple, common-fellow type, and now we are paying dearly for that gift.*

THE FOUR HORSEMEN OF THE APOCALYPSE

When does a person sleep best? According to the latest scientific report, a person enjoys his deepest sleep before 5:25 A.M. At 5:25 A.M. the average citizen is awakened, whimpering like a frightened animal, by an earthquake-like explosion. The unexpected cataclysm which throws him out of his bed is not made up of a single tone. The infernal noise sounds as if it were a variety of recorded tapes being played back at the same time: you can discern in it a sudden air raid, a buffalo stampede, a thunderstorm and a column of Centurion tanks, as well as the jungle yell of the avenging Tarzan . . . At 5.25.

Everybody reacts differently to this extraterrestrial phenomenon. There are lodgers who dig in deeply under their pillows and pray fervently. Others roll off their couches and dash about their bedrooms aimlessly. This writer as a rule no sooner hears the explosion than he hurls himself on his little wife, strangling her without uttering a single word, until she succeeds in turning on the bedside lamp and convincing him that he is not having a nightmare.

"How could a mere four men make such an infernal racket?" my neighbor Felix Selig asked, leaning out of the window at 5:25 A.M. "How?"

We watched from up there the Four Horsemen of the Apocalypse: the driver of the municipal garbage truck, the fellow who stands on the running board and the two individuals who drag out the garbage cans from the courtyard. At first sight they are four simple sanitation experts, but their unassuming exteriors conceal a quartet of top-flight virtuosi of the noise technique. The driver, for instance, drives exclusively in first gear, revving his diesel engine to the maximum, while the cans are dragged over the largest rocks in the courtyard, amid ceaseless altercations, frequently giving the impression that a terrible killing is imminent.

But by listening carefully, we found that there was no quarrel in progress. The men were chatting about the most common everyday subjects. According to the unwritten rules of disturbing the peace, the conversation begins only when the two toilers are dragging the dumpsters from deep inside the courtyard, about twenty to thirty paces from the truck. They then turn back and roar in the general direction of the driver: "Hey! Hey! Where'd you go last night, where'd you go?"

The driver sticks his head out of the window and trumpets into the rosy dawn: "Hey! We stayed at home! And you?"

"We went to the war movie, we did! It was a great movie, so help me. What acting!"

The unfortunates who live in the rear of the house swear that the two can-carrying individuals sometimes converse with each other two feet apart.

"Listen," they roar at the top of their lungs, "it's damn heavy today, damn heavy, right?"

"Of course it's heavy, they eat like horses on this street. Boy, how they eat!"

Mrs. Kalaniot, whom fate has placed plumb on top of the garbage cans and who is therefore permanently on the verge of a nervous breakdown, tore open her window one dawn and shouted at the Horsemen: "Quiet, for goodness' sake! Quiet! Why must you be so noisy every night?"

"Night, what night?" one individual roared back pleasantly. "It's already half past five, isn't it?"

"I'll call the police!" Adalbert Toscanini joined the choir of protestors, whereupon the Four Horsemen broke into such a horse laugh that any policeman passing by would have frozen into a column of salt.

"Yeah, call one, go ahead!" they roared at Adalbert. "Where are you going to find a cop at five thirty, where are you going to find one?"

They are gay, uninhibited fellows, these municipal sanitation employees, muscular Jewish boys full of vitality, *joie de vivre* and decibels. Karl Marx would have wept for joy had he lived to see them. You get the impression that no force in the world could curb them. It's an impression borne out by fact. Take ourselves, for instance. At last week's protest meeting the neighbors entrusted me with contacting the municipal sanitation department with the aim of attenuating the matutinal earthquakes. I dialed the department head and told him my tale of woe.

"You're telling me," the head replied with much feeling. "I get the same thing every morning. They're driving me nuts."

In summer, when all the windows were open, we forwarded a multi-signature petition to the authorities, in which we requested that the Four Horsemen of the Apocalypse be forbidden to toss the garbage cans three yards high in the air, thereby setting off a report which at 5:30 A.M. causes multiple nerve-snappings among the residents. We got no reply. The Sieglers' maid, a certain Etroga, who happens to live next door to the man on the running board, advised us not to do anything; two Ministers had already tried to intervene, but in the end had been forced to resign and retire to a kibbutz.

The lawyer whom we consulted considered carefully the various alternatives open to us.

"Spend the weekend in Jerusalem," he advised in the end. "There the sanitation workers frequently go on strike."

So we resorted to cotton wool. We stuffed our ears with it and achieved a certain sordino effect, but the siren-like "Heys" cut through it like a hot knife through margarine.

At the last meeting Dr. Wasserlauf gave a visionary lecture. "The chronic insomnia as well as the perpetual traumatic shocks will eventually leave their imprint on our brain functions," he said. "I have no doubt whatsoever that our heirs will show the alarming signs of their parents' degeneration and that the morning trash collection will in the final analysis result in a steep decline in the intellectual level of the general population."

Before our mind's eye appeared our grandchildren fastening on us sad, reproachful looks, then disappearing, with queer, goat-like hops into the dense forest. "No!" We ground our teeth. "Something has to be done. Something!" Siegler quoted the famous adage: "If you can't break them, join them!" This compromise attitude was in tune with our inborn sense of decency, since it goes without saying that deep in our hearts we boundlessly admired the four garbage operatives who at crack of dawn were already engaged in heavy physical work while we, poor white trash that we are, went on snoring under our blankets until 5:25. We therefore decided to try the individual psychological approach – money was no object.

On that bizarre Tuesday morning, for instance, we monitored the following broadcast.

"Hey," the running-board man roared to the others, "it's getting cold, isn't it?"

"Hey!" the reply thundered back from the recesses of the yard. "Buy yourself a sweater. A sweater buy yourself."

"What sweater! What are you saying? A sweater you say? Where have I got a sweater, hey, hey?"

We acted without further delay. For our families, for our children's future, for peace in the Middle East. Out of the house sanitation fund, Mrs. Kalaniot bought a remarkable red sweater of the largest neck size and Felix Selig, accompanied by Etroga, took it to the house of the running-board fellow. The delegation solemnly handed over the residents' gift, voicing the hope that the warm clothing would contribute toward the creation of a quieter atmosphere. The running-board fellow could hardly conceal his emotion, expressed his gratitude for the nice present and promised at once to tell his collaborators.

Next day at 5:25 Mrs. Kalaniot was hurled out of her bed by the following roar: "Hey!" boomed the running-board buffalo. "They bought me a sweater here. You hear what they bought?"

"They're nice folks, they are, nice!" the driver roared back into the daybreak. "They're good people, really good!"

Then followed the ultimate explosion when the running-board fellow, in his joy over the new sweater, hurled a garbage can in a daring parabola straight onto another can precariously balanced on the fence and the two of them richocheted onto the pavement like two stray grenades. Ever since, the hearing in my left ear is somewhat impaired. On the other hand, I sleep rather well on my right side. This is such an excellent solution that I am surprised I didn't think of it before.

The Last of the Craftsmen

One evening last week the wife looked at me as I was about to go out and said, "Why don't you have a briefcase to carry your papers in, like any self-respecting person?"

"So help me, you are right, woman," I answered. "My status as wielder of the pen certainly demands it."

"Go," the wife said, "and buy something special."

I went to the corner leather store and explained to the shopkeeper that I was looking for a special leather briefcase, something very impressive, black with a dull finish and lots of compartments, shiny locks and things. The shopkeeper was a little man who spoke only Yiddish and was not blessed with particularly good taste.

"A briefcase is a briefcase and not a jewel," he declared. "I can give you, sir, only what I've got, a very strong briefcase for Sh.55. If you want all sorts of gewgaws go and find yourself some artisan who's still got patience to talk to clients."

I was deeply insulted. Yes, I wanted first-class craftsmanship, but to say that I was looking for gewgaws? Woe to Jewish craftsmanship if this was one of its representatives. I left the Levantine merchant to his own devices and went to look for a leather artist who had learned his craft in a civilized part of Europe. After a week's frantic searching I was lucky to locate Sigmund Wasserperl, the famous fancy leather-goods maker.

As soon as I entered the workshop I could smell the sharp fragrance of cleanliness and order. Next to a large worktable I spotted a pleasant blue-eyed and white-maned oldster. It was Mr. Wasserperl in person. I described my delicate situation – naturally in Goethe's and Chancellor Kohl's language – and he listened attentively. Then the respected artist informed me that for humanitarian reasons he was ready to undertake the job and would do his best to impart to the product a character befitting my status as fellow artist. What's more, to allay my doubts as to his professional ability, Mr. Wasserperl described to me in detail his past life, starting with his graduation from the Stuttgart Government High School and including the fateful moment when it came to him like a flash of lightning that his life would be completely devoid of meaning unless he learned to make fancy leather goods. At first Mr. Wasserperl apprenticed himself with the Singer and Singer firm in Hamburg, then he moved to the famous Viennese firm of Kirschner Lederwaren and worked there – in his words – for thirty-four fruitful years.

I chatted with Mr. Wasserperl until about midnight. In the end we remembered that as a matter of fact I had come about a briefcase, and the craftsman calculated the dimensions of my future briefcase with a slide rule and logarithmic tables. Then we went on to discuss what leather would meet the demands of outer perfection and resistance to torque.

"What's your opinion on burnished buffalo hide?" Mr. Wasserperl asked.

"That's it," I answered. "I like that. Let it be burnished by all means."

"I'm really happy," Mr. Wasserperl breathed, greatly relieved. "It's a very strong hide which suits itself particularly well to ornamental embossing."

By then my initial enthusiasm had dampened somewhat. Also, I had not eaten for six hours.

"I don't want any gewgaws, you know." I tried to bring the old man back to earth, but Mr. Wasserperl interrupted me with an impatient wave of his hand.

"No second-rate workmanship is done here," he flared up. "My thirty-four years with the firm of Kirschner Lederwaren place a heavy responsibility on me. All I'm asking for is a little patience. Your briefcase will be ready day after tomorrow and the price is Sh.65."

Two days later I went to collect the briefcase, but it was not yet ready. What's more, Mr. Wasserperl had not even started working, because during two sleepless nights he had come to the decision that buffalo hide would, after all, not be suitable since it was a little too porous and he would do better to use gazelle or zebu hide, which were perhaps a little more expensive, but on the other hand they should last 100 to 150 years. Then and there I agreed to hammered zebu hide and we parted.

Three days later I came to collect my briefcase but learned from Mrs. Wasserperl that the old man had travelled early in the week to a fine mechanics factory to order the special round-headed studs made of hardened brass with which he intended to fasten the fringes of the briefcase. I told her I didn't want any studs – life was too short for that; we have to enjoy every minute of it – whereupon Mrs. Wasserperl retorted that her husband belonged to a vanishing breed of craftsmen who would rather stop working altogether than create a poor product, like those Israeli quacks. She took the opportunity of reminding me that her husband had worked for thirty-four years for the firm of Kirschner Lederwaren, who were court purveyors to His Imperial Majesty Franz Josef of the House of Hapsburg.

Gradually I resigned myself to the thought that I would end my life as a writer without portfolio. But one misty morning Mr. Wasserperl showed up in our apartment. The old man looked alarmingly tired and worried and complained bitterly that at his age he had to scour the country for a few stupid studs, while in Vienna such accessories could be found in every shop. The artist's very appearance was a mute accusation of humanity as a whole. As a matter of fact, Mr. Wasserperl had come to talk about the lining of the briefcase. He thought that only stained unicorn hide would do in view of the extraordinary resistance to wear of this rare material.

"My dear Mr. Wasserperl," I said to him, "I really appreciate your professional standards – after all, thirty-four years with Kirschner Lederwaren are not to be sneezed at – but so help me, I really don't need such a unique briefcase. Knowing my little wife, before long I'll be bringing vegetables home in it."

The old man's face lit up. "I am glad you warned me. If so, we'll have to see to it that the briefcase is waterproof both inside and out. Under the circumstances I'll line the briefcase with sheared sealskin. Have you, sir, any relations in Canada?"

"Listen, Wasserperl," I said, "a briefcase is a briefcase and not a jewel! Why don't you just finish the bloody thing and be done with it?"

"I simply can't," the deeply injured craftsman explained. "Do you think it's easy for me? And, since you mention it, how do you think, sir, that I can satisfy all your whims for Sh.65? Who will compensate me for all the time I'm wasting on this?"

Then I noticed that the poor old guy had become a nervous wreck; his face was twitching and he resembled nothing so much as a dried prune. I dispatched an urgent cable to my Uncle Egon in America and asked him to airmail me a whole sealskin. A fortnight later I cleared the parcel through customs. I hurried with the skin to Mr. Wasserperl. To my great satisfaction the old man was in a good mood, since during a quick trip to the Negev he had purchased from a couple of Bedouin shepherds some jute rope twine interwoven with gold braid with which he intended to fashion the briefcase straps. But when the old man noticed Uncle Egon's parcel he blanched and his knees started knocking.

"Plastic!" the old artist whispered, unspeakable disgust on his face. "They dare to bring plastic to Wasserperl!"

The craftsman tossed the material into the garbage can, walked to the cupboard and without saying another word took out an antique hunting rifle. Then he threw a scornful glance at me and stomped out of the workshop. His wife shouted desperately after him, but he went on, head erect and straight-backed until his tragic figure was swallowed up in the noon darkness.

"He is now going to hunt in the desert." The woman broke into bitter sobs: "I know him. He can't work otherwise. That's one of the reasons why they liked him so much at Kirschner Lederwaren."

"Thirty-four years," I reminisced, somewhat shaken, but my

sincere sympathy only poured salt on Mrs. Wasserperl's wounds.

The old woman fell on me. "Why do you torture my husband? Do you want to kill him for your silly briefcase?"

"Yes," I said. "One of these days I'll kill him."

During these troublesome days I seriously entertained the idea of knocking him off because I too had worn myself out in the struggle for the briefcase. But on that Tuesday I got a message which shook me to the depths of my soul: Mr. Wasserperl had been hospitalized in a critical condition. Afflicted with deep pangs of conscience, I bought a big bunch of flowers, put it in my new briefcase, which I had bought for 55 shekels from the corner leather store, and went to visit my victim. At the hospital I learned that somewhere on the Red Sea coast Mr. Wasserperl had shot the close relation of a seal, but the rainy weather and the exertions of the trip had overtaxed his strength and he had arrived home burning with fever. His wife was now sitting next to his sickbed and the two of them looked at me accusingly. Mr. Wasserperl was as yellow as a piece of old parchment and his eyes were bloodshot. He motioned me to bend over him. I pressed my ear against his mouth.

"You'll have ... to find ... silver clasps...." the old man whispered. "I won't agree to copper clasps. They are not suitable."

"Yes, Granddad," I whispered back. "I'm listening."

"Also," he continued with his last strength, "you'll have to get some swan dung. It's the best thing for burnishing leather."

"Everything," I promised. "I'll do everything, Granddad, I'll devote my remaining years to our briefcase, only you get well quickly."

The old man spoke no more and sank back on his pillow, completely exhausted. Full of remorse, I hurried to the head physician, with Mrs. Wasserperl's tearful curses speeding me through the hallway. The doctor explained to me that he could do nothing at present. All the patient's wishes must be fulfilled to raise his spirits. Because – that's what the doctor had learned from a reliable source – Mr. Wasserperl had been with a certain firm in Vienna and he would rather die than do a shoddy job. I asked him to pass the hospital bills on to me. Tomorrow I am going up to the northern swamps to see about swan dung. I am still young and able to work.

☐ *Many of our national difficulties stem from the fact that in their time, all the installations of our ministate were planned for 500,000 inhabitants, half of them rabbis, while today we number — even at the height of the searing hot summer, when about a third of our people flee abroad — several million souls in the shade, including influenza patients. Our cities' streets were laid out for lively bicycle traffic, the ports for motorboats, and Lod Airport for the Haifa–Tel Aviv express train. No wonder then that from time to time we run into snags which were not at all unexpected.*

WIDE-OPEN SKIES

———☐———

Gusti was sitting before the console in the airport control tower, reading a sports paper. Or so it seemed to the casual observer. In fact, hidden among the pages of the paper was the brochure: "How to Control Air Traffic in 20 Easy Lessons."

"Better play it safe," Gusti said to himself.

The day before yesterday, after a real disaster had been avoided only by a miracle, he had almost been reprimanded by the Inquiry Committee. On that occasion an aircraft — it happened to be Belgian — failed to spot the power plant smokestack over the clouds and — *boing* — smashed into it. One of its wings dropped onto a twin-engined plane flying by mistake just below, but the pilot of the small plane kept his head. By a brilliant maneuver he landed on an airliner coming from Teheran and both plummeted to the Bloomfield football stadium, almost killing Spiegel. Only ten yards separated them from the star player on the 16-meter line. Had the center forward's pass been a little longer, a real tragedy would have occurred.

Gusti looked irately at the big clock on the wall. No one had told him that this was not the radar, and up until the other day he had directed airport traffic by the second hand, which, it will be remembered, moves all the time around the clock face. As a matter of fact, the real radar had already been officially ordered in the U.S. and just as soon as the airport started to make money they would even get around to purchasing it. For the time being, a man was sent every morning from the Labor Exchange to the top of the Shalom Tower, from where he flagged down the incoming planes with a red rag. But this morning the Labor Exchange had again sent someone who spoke no Hebrew, and he kept signaling in Bulgarian.

"What a pain in the neck," Avigdor groused in another corner of the control tower. "That Pan American pilot has been pestering me for half an hour for permission to land."

"What's his height?" Gusti asked.

"Six feet in his socks."

"Consult the chart," Gusti said, "and don't bother me with such trifles."

Avigdor started leafing through the instructions. "What do they expect me to do," he complained. "They sent me here yesterday just to replace Grinspan, who is down with the flu. It's only for a few days anyway."

"Have you completed a course?"

"Not yet. But you see, I work on a chicken farm, so they thought fowls, birds, planes – you know."

A tremendous explosion came from the runway and a column of black smoke rose heavenward.

"Oh hell," Gusti remarked. "We're going to catch it again."

He hung the yellow balloon meaning "Be back soon" out the window and went to have a snack. Altogether it had been a hard day. At lunchtime two big planes had approached from the sea and by mistake had intercepted the broadcast of a radio ham from Rishon-le-Zion, and since then they were circling Tel Aviv with their wheels locked, unable to separate.

Gusti had contacted the Siamese. "No sweat, Carry on circling."

"And what if we run out of fuel?"

"Let's cross our bridges when we come to them."

Gusti immediately called the Minister of Transport on the green line and demanded an urgent inquiry committee. In the meantime things had quietened down on the airfield, since the chief meteorologist had declared a go-slow strike, and only on the intervention of the state President did he consent to announce that the weather was fair. The driver of the hay wagon which had ambled onto the runway two days before was still looking for the exit. Avigdor rang his wife at home to ask whether there was anything on TV tonight. Someone cut in on the conversation and babbled something about lights.

"Get off," Avigdor roared into the receiver. "Get off, man, get off!"

"I'm taking off. Over!" the Air France pilot replied. "But something is landing exactly opposite—"

"I'll call you back later." Avigdor took leave of his wife and returned to the pilot. "What were you saying?"

"I'm on a collision course. What shall I do?"

"Watch out," Avigdor warned. "Be careful!"

Here Rishon-le-Zion came in and broadcast light music.

Gusti came running in from the kiosk. "The rain washed out the beacon on top of the tower," he announced. "Three are flying without lights at the same height. We'll have to act immediately!"

And without further delay he dialed for an ambulance and the wrecker truck. Gusti called Inquiry Committee HQ and asked for the van, so that the committee members should be present during the triple crash. But in the end only two met in the air. The third plane was warned off in the nick of time by a dentist who got on the line, and the plane landed safely on Ben Yehuda Street, corner of Nordau Avenue.

The neighbors immediately started ringing the Minister of Transport.

"It's the second time this week," they complained. "We can't get any sleep in this racket."

The Transport Minister set up an inquiry committee. Customs set up shop on Ben Yehuda Street and began checking the luggage. In the meantime the two locked airplanes had dropped into the sea, but strollers on the esplanade thought this was an air display and cheered. The inquiry committee went out in boats. Rishon-le-Zion went off the air. The meteorologist renewed his strike. But as a whole, it was a quiet day, thank God.

☐ *According to Jewish ethics, nothing is more shameful than the inability to make a living. Better a living which doesn't bring in a penny than a remunerative job which is just a job. But this paradox can be understood only by a professional Jew.*

LIVING OUT OF A SUITCASE

The peddler first showed up at our house three years ago. He climbed the stairs, rang the bells of all the apartments, and whenever a door opened a crack, he lifted his little suitcase a few inches off the floor and asked, "Soap? Razor blades?"

He was told, "No, thanks."

"Nylon toothbrush?"

"Thanks, no."

"Plastic combs?"

"No!"

"Toilet paper?"

At that point the door would be slammed in his face. Since then the peddler has come without fail once every fortnight, rung bells, reeled off his spiel, doors have slammed shut and life has returned to normal. Once – prompted by humanitarian considerations – I tried to give him a few agorot, but the peddler refused indignantly – "I'm not a beggar, sir!" – and shot an angry glance at me.

On the day before yesterday, he showed up again on my doorstep.

"Soap?" he inquired. "Razor blades?"

A wave of furious recklessness suddenly swept over me.

"All right," I said. "Give me a razor blade."

"Nylon toothbrush?" the peddler continued.

"I said give me a razor blade."

"Plastic comb?"

"Don't you understand?" I flared up. "Give me a razor blade!"

"What?"

"A razor blade!"

An expression of boundless amazement spread over his face.

"Why?"

"A new razor blade. I – want – to buy – from you – now – a razor blade!"

"Toilet," the peddler whimpered, "paper...."

Wrenching the suitcase out of his hands, I opened it. It was utterly empty. There was nothing in it.

"What's this?"

The peddler was very angry.

"No one ever buys anything from me!" he shouted and his face grew red. "So why should I drag all this stuff along?"

"I see," I tried to calm him. "But – then – why – do you go from door to door?"

"One has to earn a living somehow, sir!"

And with that he took his leave, climbed another flight of stairs and rang the Seligs' doorbell.

☐ "Collectivism is a great theory. The only trouble with it i[s that it can]ever be realized," a witty person once said, and how right I was. [...in] microcosm, the kibbutz.

I think this is as good an opportunity as any other to relate my experiences during that gay weekend when, accepting my friend Shimon's invitation, I visited his kibbutz in order to forget amidst nature's majestic quiet the clatter and noise of the smoke-filled city.

A WIFE FOR IZZY

———□———

Shimon was overjoyed to see me, because just on that day he had moved into a new room, his little boy was down with the measles,[1] his wife was midwifing a reluctant cow, and he himself had to hurry to the dining hall where the members' plenary meeting was to discuss the case of Crazy Izzy, who for the last couple of days had been pestering them for Sh.400, or else.

"What does a kibbutznik need money for?" I asked as I ran behind Shimon toward the dining hall.

With bucolic outspokenness Shimon, who is the kibbutz treasurer, answered, "To buy himself a wife." He then gave me a running commentary on the quite unbelievable affair.

It seems that Crazy Izzy had been appointed kibbutz buyer, and had in that capacity called at one of the neighboring villages and fallen head over heels in love with a Yemenite girl named Hefziba.

That his family name was Kraus and Hefziba's Habivel did not deter him in the least. He presented himself to bearded Mr. Habivel and put into words his most honorable intentions toward his daughter.

The father of the would-be bride gave his unreserved consent,

[1] This, too, is one of the principles of collectivism: if one child goes down with German measles, all have to follow suit.

and not only that, but in view of the groom's extreme youth, did not demand for her more than Sh.400 (in cash).[2]

Izzy was flabbergasted, but the old man patiently explained that as a father he was entitled to a refund of the money he had invested in his daughter, plus a certain interest (for the risk he had incurred of the girl's dying or running away from home). In short, Crazy Izzy found that prices were fixed and went home to the kibbutz.

Now, what does a city dweller do in such cases? He takes out a construction loan, or sells his grandmother's family heirlooms, or does overtime and empties the firm's safe.

But what can a kibbutz member do? He has nothing to sell except his clear conscience, which could fetch at the most Sh.50 or 60. He can only appeal to the kibbutz secretariat for money to buy a wife.

After deliberating for only a few minutes, the secretariat rejected Crazy Izzy's request as unrealistic, for three reasons: (a) One does not buy a wife for money; (b) We are not living in the Stone Age; (c) Who ever heard of such a thing?

The secretariat on the other hand undertook to contact the aforenamed Habivel and in a matter of minutes explain to him the unwisdom of his outlook.

The kibbutz secretary and the chairwoman of the social committee therefore called on the old Yemenite, and after a day and a half came back and said that ... in fact ... if one got down to the crux of the matter ... seen from the Yemenite's point of view ... one must admit that there was something in Habivel *père*'s demand – but the price was absolutely exorbitant! (For 400 shekels one could buy a milch cow or a diesel pump!)

Crazy Izzy kicked up a terrible row and demanded that Hefziba be immediately purchased or, upon his life, he would leave these tightfisted misers and start a new life and a flower farm in the nearby

[2]The goateed immigrants from the Yemen are not only two thousand years behind our times, but extremely conservative as well. Nobody has ever succeeded in making them drop any ancient custom that is to their advantage. One of these is the selling into marriage – for a fixed price – of their daughters.

village.

"Keep your shirt on, will you!" the kibbutz leaders had said, trying to soothe him, and had convened an urgent meeting, as I related at the beginning of this story.

The atmosphere was tense. The men took up positions in the first rows, the girls lined the walls, knitting warm sweaters, and the children would not come down from the windows and go to bed. ("You want to be spanked?" "Yes, I want to be spanked.") In ominous silence the kibbutz secretary mounted the speaker's rostrum.

"*Haverim,*" he began, "we are facing an unprecedented problem. Izzy wants four hundred shekels, because that's the price of his bride. We all know that Izzy is a veteran member and a good worker. I therefore propose to cover his expenses by a grant of two hundred shekels, with the other two hundred to be given him as a twenty-year loan."

This brought Crazy Izzy to his feet.

"I don't want any favors from you, stinkers! To marry, that's almost a biological necessity, so consider me sick, see?"

"Just a moment!" The chairwoman of the health committee interrupted him. "Couldn't you look for medicine among the girls of our kibbutz?"

"Hear! Hear!" The knitting backbenchers seconded her.

Izzy completely lost his temper.

"I want a girl from outside!" he boomed. "I won't even hear of getting one without money. And not below four hundred either. Take it or leave it!"

The secretary nervously pounded the table.

"*Haverim, haverim,*" he said, "this is an emotional crisis which must be resolved by heroic means. I therefore propose that the kibbutz raise its contribution to two hundred and fifty shekels and the rest be collected among the members."

"What next!" cried the girls. "Not an agora! Let him make a fund drive in America."

At that fatal moment, Treasurer Shimon requested permission to speak, and asked a simple question: exactly from which budget would the honorable secretary take the Sh.200?

The secretary mumbled something about there being all kinds of possibilities . . . ways will be found . . . let's cross our bridges one at a time . . . etc.

"Perhaps from the development budget?" a well-meaning member volunteered, but his suggestion was drowned in the general pandemonium that broke out.

"Out of the question!" the multitude thundered. "Shall we endanger our children's security for trifles?"

This was the straw that broke Izzy's back.

"And what about my children?" he raged. "Have they no right to be born?"

"Please, *haverim!*" The secretary pummeled the table. "We must find a way out. I think that perhaps – please don't misunderstand me, Izzy – perhaps we could take the money out of the . . . the livestock budget – don't interrupt me, Izzy – it so happens that we had just now planned to buy a . . . a . . . cow."

"Murderer!" the choir of mothers sang out. "How dare you! Playing with our children's health! Milk for our babies!"

The discussion had run into deadlock. Crazy Izzy rose, livid, and in a voice trembling with emotion demanded that the money be found by noon on the morrow, even if that meant selling a number of kibbutz girls, otherwise he was going to do something all would regret.

This reminded Shimon of a possible solution: he proposed to set up a Women's Fund, into which every bachelor would in future have to pay Sh.25 or 50 for his bride, according to weight or other criteria.

"*Haverim*" – the secretary closed the meeting – "this sounds like a good idea, but I'd like to ask the bachelors to choose their brides, if possible, from among kibbutz girls, or if they insist on girls from outside, under no circumstances to agree to such extravagant prices."

With that, we dispersed. It was not yet five o'clock when I finally lay down to sleep, and hardly seven when I started on the kibbutz pickup for peaceful Tel Aviv, with its majestic quiet.

☐ *All Israelis are struck with a dangerous mania: developing the country.*

But the Jews are lazy and slap together a house in three days, so that they can loaf about for the rest of the week.

Should the reader, under the impact of this book, decide to visit Israel, he will see with his own eyes how to this day we suffer from a chronic and incurable building fever.

If some lunatic takes it into his head to erect a town in the middle of the wilderness, nobody considers this queer. As a matter of fact we have a number of such lunatics. And towns in the middle of the wilderness, too.

THE BLAUMILCH CANAL

———◻———

In a solitary cell of the Bat Yam¹ looney bin, Casimir Blaumilch, forty-five-year-old unemployed ocarina player, was throwing a fit. Five minutes earlier the nurse had taken away from him the shoehorn with

---

¹Bat Yam boasts a lunatic asylum. To be admitted is quite an achievement. Elsewhere, if somebody started crowing, people would know that he had gone out of his mind. In Israel, one has to consider the possibility that the person in question may be a new immigrant from Tibet, speaking his native brogue. He smears spinach on his head? Who knows, this may be a Bolivian custom. A lunatic has to be a first-class showman to cause even the mildest sensation.

One early Tuesday, for instance, I was sitting on the shore of the Mediterranean, enjoying the cool fragrant breeze, when I was roused by a cross-eyed, congenial, unshaven man who asked permission to sit down next to me.

"Sorry to trouble you, sir," he said, "but I need ten shekels." I asked the stranger somewhat nervously on what article of the law he based his ten-shekel claim. My visitor nodded sympathetically and willingly furnished the requested information.

"I am a madman, sir," he announced in a quiet, reassuring voice. "You seem to be an intelligent person, so I am sure you will realize what this means. Under the law of the country I could slit your throat if I felt like it, or throttle you, or – should my morbid instincts urge me to do that – even hack you into small pieces. And what would happen to me? If worst came to worst, they would return me to the asylum from which I escaped two days ago thanks to the criminal negligence of a nurse. Here are photocopies of my notarially endorsed certificates."

which he had tried to tunnel his way out. Blaumilch was a hopeless case: half a year before, he had gone out of his mind when the authorities refused to grant him an exit visa on the pretext that he was insane.[2] Since then the wretched man has been perpetually digging tunnels toward the frontier.

Suddenly he calmed down. Night had fallen. Blaumilch quietly opened the door of his cell and slipped out. . . .

Running, he caught the bus to Tel Aviv. Arrived there, he went straight to the Solel Boneh warehouse. Nobody saw him enter the building.

This happened on Tuesday.

On Thursday morning traffic came to a standstill at the intersection of Allenby Road and Rothschild Boulevard.[3] At dawn a small tent had been set up plumb in the middle of the road, and four rusty oil

My nervousness increased by the minute. My new acquaintance's papers were quite in order, and he gave the impression of a serious businesslike man who does not talk nonsense, but carefully ponders everything he says behind his feverishly burning eyes.

"What are you waiting for, sir?" the man asked. "Haven't you got enough troubles as it is? Is it worth getting involved in such a nightmarish adventure for the sake of a few measly shekels? Believe me, sir, I myself would hate to start raving, but if you force me. . . . I shall now count up to three, when – experience has taught me – my mouth will start foaming and I shall lose control over my battered nervous system. Then, may God have mercy upon us. So here goes: one . . . two. . . ."

"Just a moment," I interrupted him. "Before we go any further, I must inform you of a fact which you seem to ignore. You see, I am not quite normal myself. I think I may now confess it – after all, we are alone – that I am a diplomaed lunatic, certified by the clinics of two European countries, a long-range amok-runner, a specialist in the vivisection of my victims. It runs in my family, you understand. . . . I always carry a rusty knife with me here under my shirt, just in case. Anyway, it was a pleasure meeting you."

My visitor grew pale and I could see that my story had deeply impressed him. When I stuck a hand inside my shirt, he ran off into the dusk, shouting hoarsely.

I rose and strolled over to the bus stop. "Stand aside! I'm crazy!" I shouted at the people standing in line there. I got into the bus without queuing and rode home.

[2]We are the only country in the world that grants entry visas to lunatics, but never again lets them out – lest they bring shame on our heads.

[3]This is a spot which can be compared with Grand Central Station on a Sunday night, except that it is rather livelier.

drums announced that men were at work. At 6 A.M. a middle-aged worker showed up, dragging a brand-new, petrol-driven pneumatic drill. At 6:30 he started it up and broke the roadbed in a yard-wide X connecting the four corners of the crossroads. After that he went for breakfast.

By 10 A.M. pandemonium was complete. The line of honking cars had reached the suburbs. Mounted policemen were galloping about, barking orders left and right, but soon they too became enmeshed in the seething mechanical mass.

At noon the Minister of Police reached the site. He instructed the twenty-two high-ranking police officers present to restore order at all costs, then, shaking with anger, walked toward the municipality. Naturally, no buses were running any longer. Ambulances and fire trucks were summoned, but could not break through.

In all the infernal din only one man kept his head: the workman repairing the road. "Tatatata" went the drill in Casimir Blaumilch's strong hands, as he slowly but inexorably advanced up Allenby Road toward the sea.

The Minister did not find Dr. Kuybishev, Municipal Coordinator of Road Mending, in his office. He had gone to Jerusalem, and his deputy was rather noncommittal about the matter. All the same, he promised the Minister to have the work stopped as soon as Dr. Kuybishev returned. A telegram was dispatched to Jerusalem.

The mayor got wind of the case and ordered his secretary to make an on-the-spot investigation. The secretary walked down Allenby Road, passed the triple police cordon, approached the concrete-chewing workman, and, taking advantage of a momentary lull in the nerve-racking clatter, asked him when he thought he would be finished.

Casimir Blaumilch did not answer at first, but when he saw that he could not get rid of the tiresome individual, he threw at him the only Hebrew word he knew, *"Hamor!"*[4]

[4]Literally, this means "ass," but its true meaning is "You scatterbrained, dumb yak bullock!"

The police – with superhuman efforts, here and there using tear-gas bombs – restored a semblance of order, freed the completely exhausted mounted policemen, and barred all traffic from a half-mile stretch of Allenby Road. The municipality and the management of Solel Boneh were informed.

Two days later, upon receipt of the telegram, Dr. Kuybishev returned from Jerusalem and found his Tel Aviv office topsy-turvy. His clerks had ransacked the archives looking for the Allenby-Rothschild road-mending project. They had found two different plans and could not decide which of them was relevant.

Dr. Kuybishev asked for the two plans, and finding some reference to sewage, forwarded them to the Sewage Department, whose director was just then in Haifa on an important mission. The plans were sent to him by courier, but were returned with the remark that as there were practically no sewers in Tel Aviv, there was obviously some mistake.

In the meantime Dr. Kuybishev had been transferred to the Ministry of Commerce, and his successor, Haim Pfeiffenstein, after carefully studying the documents, marked them with a big red question mark and sent them to the Ministry of Labor, demanding to know why it had embarked on a public works project without previously consulting the municipal authorities.

Casimir Blaumilch had meanwhile reached Rambam Street. "Tatatata" he went on relentlessly, day and night, between four wandering rusty barrels, and Allenby Road dwellers dejectedly beheld their thoroughfare transformed into a desert bespattered with pieces of macadam, through which even pedestrians could make their way only with difficulty.

The greatest headache was caused by the complete disorganization of traffic, which had become practically paralyzed with the elimination of Allenby Road and Rothschild Boulevard. The side streets were heavily overburdened and had to be widened. Funds for this were provided through a government loan. The Central Bus

Station naturally had to be transferred to the north, and this necessitated the razing of the Rabbi Smuk quarter.

Haim Pfeiffenstein, having received a sharp rejoinder from the Minister of Labor, reported to the mayor, then asked Solel Boneh for information on the progress of the operation. That company's road construction manager, Piotr Amal, promised to look into the matter. Copies of the correspondence were sent to the Settlement Department of the Jewish Agency.

Piotr Amal also proposed to mediate between Tel Aviv and the Labor Ministry and informed the Histadrut executive of this decision, but the mayor demanded that the work be stopped first and informed the bus cooperatives.

Allenby Road was a picture of utter desolation. It had become a deep ditch flanked by mountains of concrete and macadam. Clouds of fine dust hovered perpetually overhead. From the damaged water mains, two-storey-high fountains spurted skyward. The neighborhood had become more or less deserted.

In this critical situation, Piotr Amal gave proof of great political wisdom. He summoned Dr. Kuybishev to his office, and after four hours of hot debate they agreed to suspend the work until a parliamentary committee could investigate the matter. Afterward they sent a circular to the State Controller and the President.

All this was actually quite superfluous. A fortnight before, Casimir Blaumilch had turned slightly to the left, and on Thursday at dawn he reached the sea.

The rest is rather commonplace.

The sea surged into the canal that had previously been Allenby Road and was soon washing the banks of Rothschild Boulevard. The city quickly realized the possibilities inherent in the new conditions. Taxi motorboats began to ply the canal, and soon private motorboats were jamming the waterway. Life returned to Allenby "Road."

At the official inauguration of the canal, the mayor expressed his thanks to Solel Boneh for its magnificent achievement in implementing the plan strictly according to schedule. He then named Tel Aviv "the Venice of the Middle East."